Zed
and the
Cormorants

Clare Owen

First published in UK 2021 by Arachne Press Limited
100 Grierson Road, London SE23 1NX
www.arachnepress.com
© Clare Owen 2021
Illustrations © Sally Atkins 2021
Chapter headers © David Anstey 2021
ISBNs
Print: 978-1-909208-87-2
ePub: 978-1-909208-88-9
Mobi/Kindle: 978-1-909208-89-6
Audio: 978-1-913665-23-4

The publication of this book is supported using public funding by the National Lottery through Arts Council England.

Thanks to Muireann Grealy for her proofing.
Cover Design © Klara Smith 2021.

Printed on wood-free paper in the UK by TJ Books, Padstow.

Zed
and the
Cormorants

For Tom, Esme, Edie & Ted

One

There was a huge bird glaring down from the roof.

It wasn't pale sea green, like the metal sculptures on the Liver Building near where Nanny Pam lived, but it had the same long neck and the same wings, angled like coat hangers. The birds in Liverpool seemed friendly though. They kept watch over the sea and the city and the football club, but this one was only watching them. And it was black.

The colour made all the difference.

Zed lifted her phone and took a picture. It turned its head, in a series of tiny jerks, like the CCTV cameras at her school. *Correction. Her old school.* She zoomed in on its profile, the hooked beak and snake-green eye, the warning flash of yellow on the side of its head.

Maybe she'd send it to Bethany, if she ever found a signal, with a caption like, 'A warm welcome from the locals!' She could see her best friend's lopsided smile, that one dimple appearing just below where her freckles stopped. She could see her so clearly, typing her reply while twisting a lock of thick dark hair around her finger, the way she always did when she was focused on her phone, that it was impossible to believe she was over two hundred and fifty miles away. Two hundred and fifty miles! She was probably doing that now. Sitting cross-legged, her elbow resting on her knee, sending endless messages out into space, into the huge blank space between them.

Messages that couldn't bridge the gap.

Zed walked backwards across the lawn, trying to fit her new home into the screen. It looked better from this side. From the road it was too close and too wide and seemed cobbled together, as if bits kept being added whenever another room was needed, but from the back garden Tremelin House was big and square and framed by trees. It had three large sash windows along the top, and two on either side of a lead porch with wrought iron posts. Up close you saw that the paint was peeling, and the windowsills were beginning to rot, but from a distance at least, it didn't seem quite so run down. 'A project,' was how Dad described it.

'I hate it here!' Amy was screaming. Again.

They'd opened all the windows to try to get rid of the musty smell and Amy's voice seemed to bounce off the wide, deep stone steps that led down from the drive. They were perfectly designed for such a purpose, like a Greek amphitheatre.

'I promised Luke I'd call at six-thirty. He'll be waiting for me. How can there be no internet? How can there be no phone signal? Why are you doing this to me?'

'Right now, the internet's not my priority,' said Dad calmly. 'Right now I want to make sure everyone has something to sleep on for the night.'

But this seemed to wind up Amy even more.

'I don't want to sleep here! I don't want to stay in this hellhole! It's the middle of nowhere. You're doing your absolute best to ruin my life!'

Dad put the vacuum down on the path and stood awkwardly in front of Zed.

For a moment she wondered if he was going to ask her what *she* thought of it. *As if.* Instead he said, 'Do you mind taking the bedding up?'

Mum was in the kitchen, if you could call it that, leaning against an old butler sink that looked more like a bath. She was clutching a large glass of wine. There were no fitted cupboards, just a filthy cast-iron range under the window and big slate flagstones on the floor. Zed had never seen a range before their holiday down here last Easter. The one in the rented cottage was dark green with shiny polished lids over the hot plates. This one was rusting and coated with a thick layer of grease and dust.

Dad came in, bouncing up and down on his toes and running his hand over his bald patch.

'Isn't it great, Lucy?' he said. 'There is so much potential. So many things we can do—'

'Well, why don't you start by putting the beds together?' said Mum. 'I'm proper shattered.'

Zed was shattered too. They'd been up early, really early, and driven all day. And Dad had gone on and on about their 'fresh start' the entire way.

'No more tasteless, cellophane wrapped, pesticide-infused vegetables for us!' he said, banging the steering wheel with the heel of his hand. 'We'll be growing our own! This is all about choosing a better way, a simpler life, breathing fresh sea air and living off the land.'

'Sea air? I thought you told us we were five miles from the beach?' said Zed.

'Five miles is nothing! Besides we're only a few hundred yards from the river.

And you can swim there. I spoke to the farmer about renting the little boathouse by the water. We can store things in it, towels, sun cream–'

Zed glanced at her sister, poised to roll her eyes, but the days when they laughed at Dad's random enthusiasms seemed eons ago. Most of Amy's face was hidden behind a curtain of super straight, blue-black hair, but the white of her one visible eye, was pink, and the thick kohl circle she'd drawn around it, even more smudged than normal. She was facing the window, but staring at nothing, lost in the lyrics of another tragic song.

'He's the one that told me all about the house,' said Dad. 'Built by a miller, apparently. Got the original bread oven too. Hasn't been used for years, but I'm going to get it started and–'

Zed shut her eyes and did her best to zone out.

*

Beth, Kabir and Caitlin understood. They were shocked and outraged when she told them. They actually saw it from her point of view.

'So, he's dragging you away, just like that? Without any discussion?' said Caitlin. 'That really sucks!'

'What? You're going for good?' Blotches of red appeared on Beth's neck. Zed watched them merge together and lurch towards her cheeks.

'Why did they even bother to let Amy sit her exams?' asked Kab. 'It's not as if she's done any work, or is going to pass any of them, she's too busy hanging out with that bunch of miserable freaks.'

'Well, I guess they needed some time to get things sorted,' replied Zed. 'And Amy did actually start doing some work. Finally. That's why they didn't tell us until now, in case she stopped again.'

She was so relieved that she'd told them, so glad she hadn't wimped out and messaged them instead, that she talked way too fast.

'Apparently, they've known since Easter, when we were on holiday down there. They sneaked off to see the house one afternoon, then sat up all night debating whether it was the right thing to do. Didn't think to talk it over with us, obviously, decided 'yes', and Dad put in an offer the next day.'

'It's about everyone else except you, isn't it?' said Beth. Zed loved the way her best friend always got it. Straight away. No messing.

'So as soon as Amy was done, they wanted to get her away from the evil Luke, and you can see their point,' said Caitlin, 'but Cornwall? It's a bit extreme isn't it?'

'Wow!' said Kab grinning. 'She might get a suntan! She might eat a pasty! She might even,' he did a drum roll on his lunch box, 'put on a pair of shorts!' He was always going on about how white and skinny Amy was. And how he'd only ever seen her wearing tight ripped black jeans. Even when she was allegedly in uniform.

'You know my dad. No half measures. Now that he's accepted redundancy, he wants to change his whole life. It's not really about him or Amy though–' Zed paused and took a deep breath. 'He's trying really hard to make Mum happy again. She had some really nice holidays down there, as a child and–'

'But do you think she'll actually go? Amy, I mean,' said Caitlin. 'Don't you think, like, she'll try and run away or something?'

'Yeah, didn't Luke want her to go and live with him in his uncle's caravan anyway?' said Kab. 'He's got big plans for them, oooh yeah, a life hanging out in a trailer, smoking spliffs and spending his dole on getting their backs tattooed!'

'And what about you?' said Caitlin. 'Just say *no!* It's really simple. They can't make you, Amy won't go, and neither should you.'

'They have to go!' said Beth. She locked eyes with Zed and the other voices faded into white noise. 'They can't risk disappointing her mum, not if it's what she wants, not after what happened. What if she tried to do it again and–'

She didn't need to finish the sentence.

Yep, as always, Beth had got it. Straight away. No messing.

*

Zed left her parents searching for a screwdriver in the kitchen, and found two pillows and her duvet in a ziplock bag by the front door. She dragged them across the wooden floor and up the stairs. There were boxes piled at the bottom, leaning against the wall, the flaps taped up with gaffer tape. There were boxes half way up, on the wide ledge under the big, arched window, and more boxes on the top landing.

Zed's room was at the far end. It was L-shaped and overlooked what the estate agents' particulars had called 'the kitchen garden', presumably because once upon a time something edible had been grown in the greenhouse or in the beds that were now a tangle of nettles and brambles. She looked at the mattress on the floor. She couldn't be bothered to go searching for a sheet, so just dumped the pillows and duvet, threw herself on top of them and stared at the ceiling. It was the same dirty yellow as the walls. There were two exposed wooden beams, bare and grimy, perfect for hanging things, though, a row of paper butterflies maybe.

She hadn't known what to get for her friends, but without really planning it she started making origami dragons just like Granny Steph had taught her when she was little. She found a stash of squares stuffed into the back of her drawer. Just one, she thought, to see if she could remember how to do it, and then another, because she didn't get the fold on the tail quite right. And another because one of the squares of paper had a design of Liquorice Allsorts (and Kab loved Liquorice Allsorts) and another because... because... Soon she had made one for everyone in her class, well at least all the ones who spoke to her and might not immediately rip them up and chuck them in the gutter. They would have probably preferred sweets or something, but hey... She made an origami box for her form tutor too, one that opened out into a rose. Miss Pearce hadn't really got it at first and just said a polite 'thank you', thinking that was it, a square green box, but when Zed showed her how you folded back the green sides to expose the red rose underneath, she clapped her hands with delight.

No one cried before registration, but after that it was tears, snot and tissues all the way. Kab didn't cry of course. He wouldn't have done himself any favours if he had, especially with Liam Marks waiting to pounce on anything he could label as 'gay', and anyway Zed would have found that too weird. And although he had tried to kiss her that time, at Jay's party, and she'd told him she'd rather stick pins in her eyes then allow him to shove his tongue down her throat (it was a miracle they were still friends really), he'd never hugged her before, so when he pulled her to him and she pressed her face into his blazer and could smell his deodorant and orange throat sweets, that was weird enough. Weird cool, but still weird.

They'd all clubbed together to buy her a really nice ink pen and a book of stamps. 'So you can actually send us, like, proper postcards. You are going to the seaside after all.'

Saying goodbye to Beth was the hardest. They went for iced coffees just the two of them, and sat outside the café long after the waitress had cleared away their glasses, neither of them wanting to be the first to leave. They gripped hands across the table, but when their fingers softened and fell apart, Zed couldn't bear it any longer.

'I don't want to go!' she wailed.

'I don't want you to leave,' said Beth, her voice cracking again.

'But I have to. You get that, right?'

Beth nodded, but now that it was crunch time, she didn't look so convinced.

'Dad thinks Mum needs a complete lifestyle change. A new chapter. We'll have lots of space and somewhere she can make her jewellery again, you know that always cheers her up. He's pretty excited about it all, and, well I guess he's been kind of depressed too, this last year, so maybe he's right. Cornwall is–'

'A place with happy memories and together you'll make a lot more?' Beth sniggered.

'If you'd said that seriously, I'd have had to think about trading you in for–'

Zed's eyes welled up. A new best friend would never be possible.

Beth was still laughing. She was so frickin' beautiful when she laughed. It just wasn't fair.

'Any more puke-inducing, feel-good advice?'

'Nah, think I'm done for now.'

'Look, it's not like we're not going to see each other ever again. You can come and stay.'

'Only if it's got a power shower and under-floor heating!'

'And I'll be up to see Granny Steph soon – just give us a few weeks to get ourselves sorted. And we *will*... get ourselves sorted. We have to. Let's face it, it's–'

'Last-chance saloon for your mum?'

'Well, yeah.' Zed stared at a screwed up napkin. 'And that's why I'm going to do my absolute best to give it a go. She's got to think that at least one of us is up for it. If she knows she's making us both miserable, she'll fall to pieces. And then–'

'Yeah, I know.'

'Do you promise?'

'What?'

'Do you promise that you understand?'

'I guess...'

'Come on Beth, pinky promise, remember?'

And the thought of linking fingers once more, even just their baby ones, for a moment, was enough to make Zed feel a bit better.

Then she got to her feet knowing this was it.

'I'm not going to hug you again,' she said with a wobbly grin, 'or message you the moment I get to the bus stop. I'm just going to walk off down the road. And you've got to do the same.' Beth stood up too. 'In the opposite direction!' said Zed. They both giggled. 'I mean it,' she said. 'Please–'

'But it's your last night – *our* last night and–'

'And what?' asked Zed, a little too quickly.

'Well, I live two streets away from you,' said Bethany.

'Then you'd better take the long route home!'

Two

Zed woke up with the sunlight. There were no blinds or curtains at the window and the first thing she felt was a warm red glow behind her eyelids. When she opened them, in the split second or two before she knew where she was, she focussed on the dust dancing around in the square streams of pale yellow light. And then – *Bam!* Cornwall. Furry teeth, and yesterday's clothes.

She pushed the duvet back, slipped on her flipflops and went downstairs. In the kitchen, the window was open and she could hear crowing, the relentless cock-a-doodle-doo of a rooster over the road. Wasn't that supposed to be your wake-up call in the country? No one else seemed to be taking any notice.

Zed yanked open the back door and wandered out into the garden. The grass was lumpy and wet with dew. On the far side of the lawn the ground fell away towards a stream and through the weeds she could just make out some flagstones marking a path down to a little wooden bridge. Her flipflops squeaked as she made her way towards two weeping willows, just like the ones on Granny Steph's favourite china teacups, their branches draped across the bank, skimming the water. She parted the curtain of branches and stepped into the space between them and the trunk, and in a moment the thin leaves rustled back into place, enclosing her entirely. It was like being inside a glistening green tent. Green was Bethany's favourite colour. She had green trainers, at least two green hoodies, a green bra...

Zed dipped her toe into the water, *Jeez,* it was cold, and as it trickled over her feet, the tingle of the nettle stings acquired on her way to the willows quickly faded into numbness. She waded out into the middle of the stream and followed it past some half-collapsed fencing, the wooden posts rotting into the reeds and two slack barbed wires lying in the mud. Outside their garden, the water got deeper and wider, so she climbed up onto a gravel path running alongside, that soon gave way to dried mud, dead leaves and twigs. It led under a huge stone viaduct, the height of at least three double-decker buses. Zed sang a few notes, as she passed under the arches. The sound swelled, but the stones, damp with gelatinous algae, didn't echo her tune as she'd hoped they would, not like in the underpass near Beth's house, where they'd always serenaded each other with gut-wrenching torch songs.

The path divided and Zed rejected a sharp right which rose steeply up the side of the hill, to continue parallel to the water as it opened into a creek, snaking its way through mud and marsh. New little trees, growing up through the ferns, were dwarfed by huge oaks. Dead branches, silver grey, were knotted with ivy and lay tangled in the undergrowth.

A large tree had fallen across the stream; it was covered in pea green moss. A family of ducks drifted around in lazy circles. Zed watched them for a moment before abandoning her flipflops in a tuft of ferns and tiptoeing up the trunk. To keep herself steady she turned ninety degrees, and she saw a low stone building by the water's edge. It must be the boathouse Dad had mentioned. As she edged her way further out, her bare feet arching over the soft bark, a crumbling slipway came into view and beyond that the stream met the wide, flat river.

She eased herself down onto her bottom, shut her eyes and tilted her face to the sun.

All at once the ducks started a frenzy of quacking and beating the water with their wings. Zed jerked back and almost lost her balance.

She heard a yelping and looking up she saw a little dog running backwards and forwards on the edge of the bank. His paws were completely covered in thick brown sludge.

'Leave them alone, Buttons!' she heard someone shout. The dog stopped scampering for a moment when he saw Zed. He put his head on one side and twitched his ears, but there was no let-up in the yapping.

'Buttons! Give it up!' commanded the voice again, then, 'Oh, it's you he'll be showing off to,' and a frail looking elderly woman appeared by the roots of the fallen tree. She was wearing a shapeless knitted jumper, the shade of blue wool changing half-way down her front, filthy wellington boots and a creamy coloured hat with a brim: the type umpires wear at a cricket match.

Zed started to shimmy back down the tree trunk on her bottom. She made slow progress over the scabby bark and at no stage did the woman stop staring.

'I bet you wish you'd worn trousers!' she said as Zed jumped down onto the path.

If there were wishes going spare, Zed could think of a few that would bump trousers down the list.

'Now, I was going to apologise for my rooster, but then I remembered your sister! She's got some lungs on her, hasn't she?'

'She doesn't want to be here,' said Zed.

'And you?'

Where to start.

'I'm Cordelia,' the woman said, thrusting out her hand, 'and that look says it all!'

Cordelia's hair was white, completely straight and cut into a short bob, not entirely level. Close up, Zed could see how old she was. Her face was covered in wrinkles and patches of darker brown skin, especially on her forehead and cheeks. Were those the age spots that Mum feared? Well, they weren't so bad, they just looked like freckles that had joined together in clusters; a safety in numbers kind of thing.

'And you are?'

'Zed. Well, it's actually short for–'

'Hmm. Good,' she said and started off down the path. 'You coming then? You can throw some sticks for Buttons. That's the quickest way to shut him up.'

They left the path and picked their way across a squelchy marsh of thick grasses that dropped onto oozing mud.

'You know, this river used to be as busy as the A30. It was the main route to Clewmor, and beyond of course, and all sorts were taken up and down: quarried stone, tin, slate. You'd never guess to look at it now, would you?'

'Clewmor. Is that the nearest town?'

'Twenty minutes by boat. If you get the tides right.'

'And by car?'

'Well you can't drive, can you?' said Cordelia, 'so that's irrelevant! And your parents won't want to be ferrying you about. You'll need to get places under your own steam!'

'Dad mentioned renting out the boathouse.'

'Mmm – well, Dicky has cleared it all out. I know that much. Dropped a few bits round to mine, things he thought I might make use of. He's got a grandson getting wed so, price of milk an' all that, I guess he had to put aside any qualms–'

'Qualms?'

'He needs the money!' She took a deep breath, 'And it's about time too, I suppose. Can't stay empty forever.'

'Empty?' asked Zed, who'd been hoping it housed a speedboat.

'No one's used it for seventy years,' said Cordelia. 'Dicky's done a few repairs now and then, but that's it. He's a funny chap. Cornish through and through. Never crossed the Tamar, and they're full of stories of spriggans, piskies and knockers, those that have never left.'

'Spriggans?' said Zed. 'Piskies?'

'Yes. And ghosts, of course.' Cordelia turned and marched back towards the path.

'Not standing there for long,' she hollered. 'Holes in my boots!'

'Aren't you Cornish then?' Zed called after her.

'Oh, I was born in the farm on top of the hill, but I lived in other places too,' she shouted over her shoulder. 'Bristol, when my daughter was little, but she wanted to come back down here to raise her child. My husband had died by then, so I followed her.'

Zed was struggling to keep up in her wet flipflops.

'Not much changed while I was away, but I was shocked to discover that the boathouse had been empty all that time. Didn't seem right. I mean, I can understand that no one would want to live there – after what happened, and of course it was never built to be lived in, but to not even store a boat in it?' Cordelia trailed off.

'Blow-ins there too!' she said, when they got back to the road. She was pointing at the squat little cottage.

'Blow-ins?'

'Second homers! Probably only visit two or three times a year. That's more than the last lot who lived in your house though. And at least they've given theirs a lick of paint.' She looked up sharply. 'You're not second homers, are you? Not with all that stuff?'

'No,' replied Zed with a sigh. 'We're here full time.'

'Course you are,' Cordelia nodded with approval. 'Hence all the shouting.' Then she added, 'She sounds like a proper madam, your sister.'

'Maybe it's harder for her than for me,' said Zed.

'Nonsense,' came the reply.

They had reached Tremelin House and while Zed wrestled with the rusty gate Cordelia said, 'The boathouse was just right for Gawen. He was a fisherman, so it was perfect really, right by the water. And Kerra would have made a lovely little home there, but it was not to be.'

'Kerra,' said Zed slowly rolling it around in her mouth. 'Gawen. They have very unusual names down here.'

'Ha!' said Cordelia. 'That's rich coming from you!'

With that, she raised her arm in a wave, turned and shuffled over the road to her front door.

Mum was making breakfast in the kitchen.

'Oh,' she said, 'I didn't know you were up. How did you sleep in your new room?'

Dad ran in carrying a red metal toolbox.

'Look what I've found!'

Mum took the toast off the range and buttered the thick slices before handing one to Zed and one to Dad.

'No thanks,' he said. 'I'll hold out for the proper stuff.'

14

'It's not that bad,' said Zed.

'Mmm – not square and pre-sliced, but it's still mass-produced and squashed into polythene! Now, come on. Let's go and find Mum's studio.'

They went out into the garden and up the steps to where the car was parked. Beyond this were the outbuildings. There was a woodshed and a stable, then a building with a lower roof, but when they pushed the door open it was filled with light, the back wall having been almost entirely replaced with glass. Laid out on a bench were Mum's wire cutters, pliers, a soldering torch and her wooden dapping block. Dad put down the toolbox and flicked open the catch, to reveal the three tiers of compartments filled with beads and coloured stones.

'What do you think?' he asked nervously.

They heard footsteps outside.

'I got a signal!' said Amy, as she threw herself against the doorframe. She was out of breath, but almost smiling. 'At the top of the hill, by the gate to the farm, there were three bars.'

'Well done, love,' said Mum. 'Did you call anyone?'

Big mistake.

Amy scowled. 'Duh– course I did.'

'And how is he?' asked Mum.

'As if you care!' Amy yelled and then stormed off back down to the house.

Zed spent the rest of the morning unpacking her bedroom. Lots of her things were wrapped in newspaper and when a pile of it built up in the corner of her room it gave her an idea. Papier maché. She would blow up balloons and make masks to cover her wall. Happy masks. She'd shape smiles and laughter lines, gaping, giggly mouths. Ironic? Maybe – but only she would know!

She looked into Amy's room to ask her not to throw any newspaper away, but Amy was lying on her bed staring at the wall. She hadn't opened a single box.

Dad was up by the outbuildings.

'Can you put wallpaper paste on your shopping list?'

'Ask Mum, she's in charge of all that,' he said. 'But come see this – it's a beauty.'

The Old Bakery had a concrete floor and a high ceiling with thick grey beams. In the far corner, opposite the door, was the oven, covered in cobwebs. The bottom half was square and made of large chunks of stone, and above it tapered up into a kind of dome.

'Go on, look inside!' said Dad, pointing to the semi-circular opening. 'That's the baking chamber.' He was skipping from one foot to the other like a little boy. 'Yes, it's about wanting us to be more self-reliant, but I'm also going to do my best to make a business out of this. Artisan baking. And we can do it how they did. Use wood from the garden, bake every day and boat the bread up to Tremarrak and down to Clewmor. No traffic, no fuel costs, no chemicals.' He paused for a moment. 'Exciting, eh?'

'If you say so, Dad.'

There was a box of eggs on the back doorstep. Zed bent over to pick them up and the door across the road swung open to reveal a girl in a tight red t-shirt, cut-off denim shorts and trainers. She leaned against the frame with her arms crossed, and stared at Zed. She had a wrist thick with friendship bands, but didn't seem that friendly.

'There's lots more where they came from,' she said. 'She sells them in the little box by the fence.'

'Oh, I'll er – get some money.'

'They're a present!' she snapped, flicking back a choppy blonde fringe. 'Housewarming, apparently.'

'Thank you. Um – how many chickens has she got?' Zed cringed, hoping it didn't sound as idiotic as she thought. No such luck.

'Ooh, well, let's see, twenty or so,' the girl replied with a fake chirpy voice, '– an' two goats, four cats, a dog an' a roof full of bats.'

Zed laughed.

'It's no laughing matter,' she scowled. 'They crap everywhere.'

'Do you live here as well?'

'You must be joking. I live in Clewmor with my dad. I'd go nuts out here.'

'Well, thanks, that's encouraging!' said Zed.

'Seriously, I doubt you'll be able to put up with it for long. We see it all the time. People rock up, think, *yeah – I wanna bit of this. It's sooo idyllic. There's no commute and we can turn a hobby into our living, we'll get fit and de-stress,* blah, blah, blah – an' they don't last five minutes.'

'Well that's not us!' said Zed. She hoped she sounded more confident than she felt.

'It's not like on the TV.'

'I know that!' said Zed.

'It rains. A lot.'

'It rains in cities too!'

'Sure, but it can be bleak out here, just you wait. Does weird stuff to your head. You lot who think you can move down here for good, you're worse than the second homers. At least they know that they can only hack it in August!'

'Well, maybe we're not like everyone else.'

'Talk to her,' said the girl, ignoring Zed and jerking her thumb back inside the cottage. 'She's my great-gran, but the two generations between us have scarpered. My gran ran away to Sydney, about as far from here as she could get, and her daughter – well, you ask Cordelia what it did to my mum.'

Zed didn't know what to say.

'Seriously, you should ask her!'

'Um–'

'Well, maybe best not. Look, I'm outta here.' She sauntered off around the side of the house and came back a moment later wheeling a bike. 'See you around, I guess.' Then she added under her breath, but loud enough for Zed to hear, 'If you don't end up topping yourself.'

Now that really wasn't funny.

Zed went into the house and slammed the door.

That evening she decided to go and collect the keys to the boathouse. After all Mum had her studio and Dad had his precious bakery, and maybe things wouldn't seem so bad if she had somewhere to escape to, or at least somewhere to store the means to escape!

Amy had said there was a phone signal at the top of the hill and the first thing Zed did was call Beth.

'Hey you.' She picked up on the first ring. 'What's it like then?'

'Bit rustic for your taste. I can send you some pictures now,' said Zed, 'and all your messages have just come through. Finally!'

'And there was I thinking, out of sight, out of mind.'

That was a joke, right?

'So there's this girl across the road, a real charmer, thinks we're going to run back to London at the first opportunity.'

'Mmm, that's nice. *Not!*'

'Well, I guess it makes me want to prove her wrong.'

'No, I'm looking at your photos – and I *meant* your house!'

The farmer came out of his front door as soon as Zed turned into the drive. He marched right up close to her before saying quickly and very quietly,

'You come for this?' He glanced around before pulling a key on a chain from his pocket.

'Yes, please,' said Zed, stepping backwards.

'Not sure, as it be the right thing,' he muttered. 'You give 'em back any time you want. No need to explain.'

'I'm sure that won't be necessary,' she replied.

'No one wanted to go anywhere near,' he continued, shaking his head. 'Been a long time empty.'

'Yes, so I hear.'

'And I really don't like the place,' he said, looking at his muddy boots. 'Gives me the jitters something chronic.'

'It's only really for storing stuff, but I do need a boat, and I wondered if you might know where I could get–'

'Well, best not go down there after dark.'

Zed remembered that Dad had given her an envelope of bank notes.

'Oh,' she said, reaching into her pocket, 'this is for you.'

He shook his head again. More vigorously this time.

'We'll sort it out later. When I know that – you're all okay.'

Zed stood there awkwardly. Cordelia said he needed the money.

'Do me a favour instead,' he continued, holding out a bag and shaking it, 'I got somethin' in 'ere that I don't want. An' I know Cordelia wouldn't want it either, too many memories, but I can't bring myself to chuck it away. Seems disrespectful somehow an' you don't want to disrespect 'em! Do somethin' with it, will you? Mebbe take it to the library?'

He stuffed the bag into Zed's hand.

'They're into local history an' always looking for old photographs an' that.'

'Of course,' said Zed, taking it. 'What is it?'

The farmer wiped his hands on his trousers.

'Best leave 'er in there,' he replied gruffly, but Zed had already pulled out an old sepia photograph in a battered wooden frame. It was a bird like the one she'd seen on the roof, but scrawnier, almost bat-like if you ignored the long snakey neck and the nasty looking beak.

'What is it?' said Zed again, holding up the corner of the frame between her thumb and forefinger.

The farmer stepped back and shuddered.

'It's a cormorant!' he whispered. 'Now take it and go.'

Three

The following afternoon they all drove into Clewmor. They parked at the top of town by the Clewmor Academy. You couldn't miss the big shiny letters drilled into the wall. It was a mixture of new red brick with a sort of swanky reflective glass and pre-fabs with tatty blue fascia boards. It didn't seem much like a school, more like an abandoned office block. Zed squeezed her eyes shut and tried to imagine the place teeming with kids. Kids like Kab, Caitlin and Bethany – but it didn't work.

Standing by the ticket machine, they could see over all the roofs, to the church tower, the town quay and the pontoons in the estuary, with lines of sailing boats all pointing out to sea.

Mum and Dad were fumbling around trying to find the right change, so Zed and Amy set off by themselves, down some steps, across a road and along a steep, wide passage between rows of old stone houses, each with a different arrangement of steps to get up to their front doors. At the bottom they reached Fore Street. This was the Cornwall Zed remembered: all pasties and fudge, ice cream parlours, cafés and pubs. There were galleries and gift shops too, all selling the same carved wooden seagulls, driftwood lamps and blue and white striped crockery.

'I'm going to scout around the cafés,' said Dad when they'd caught up, 'and I've got a meeting with the head chef at Clewmor Hall at eleven thirty.'

Mum groaned.

'Shaun, you haven't actually made any bread yet! Shouldn't you at least do that before you start selling yourself as a baker?'

'Don't worry, I'm just getting to know the lie of the land. It's market research, putting the idea out there!' He grinned and rubbed his hands together. 'Now, you girls go and explore, and I'll see you in a couple of hours.'

Amy made a beeline for the nearest coffee shop and within moments she was standing at the counter, ordering herself a double espresso and typing their wifi code into her phone. Zed and Mum wandered in behind her and looked at the blackboard.

'Actually I think I might mosey around a bit first,' Mum said.

Zed looked at Amy's back. She didn't much fancy sitting in here with her sister glued to her screen, but Amy said, 'She'll have one of those deluxe hot chocolates with all the trimmings,' and that was hard to resist.

They sat in the corner. After flicking through a few group chats and posting Beth a picture of the harbour, Zed glanced at the local paper, which seemed to be mainly adverts and wedding photos full of fake ringlets, meringue dresses and rictus grins. She reached into her bag and felt her new ink pen.

'I'm just going to pop over there,' she said, pointing to the newsagent.

'Yeah. I'm done here,' replied Amy, standing up and running two fingers down her fringe.

After ten minutes of turning each of the three display racks round and around, selecting, replacing and selecting again, Zed had chosen her postcards. A man gorging on a giant pasty for Kab, a view of Clewmor in the snow for Caitlin, who always said winter was her favourite time of year, and a jigsaw for Beth, where you wrote your postcard and then broke it up into little pieces and put it in an envelope. Beth could be so impatient, for things like puzzles and crosswords anyway, and the thought of her groaning with frustration when she realised she'd have to put it together to be able to read it, made Zed smile. Amy bought a postcard too. It was of a little baby on the beach, wearing a baseball cap and shades and screaming because he'd dropped his ice cream in the sand.

'Who is that for?' said Zed.

'Me,' Amy replied.

They walked down onto the quay. There was a fat man doing caricatures and a woman with two little dogs offering to braid hair. Zed was tempted, but the price was per inch and her plait reached her lower back.

'She'll be here all summer,' said Amy, 'and it's not like you've got anything else to do!'

They wandered up the main street, buying sticks of rock from an old-fashioned sweetshop, eyeliner from the chemist and balloons from a gift shop selling an enormous collection of fridge magnets and trinket boxes made out of shells. At the end, by the post office, the road took a sharp left and set back from the pavement, up three steps, was a shop with a yellow and silver door.

'Ooh – let's have a look in here,' said Amy.

It was called Clewmor Crystals. Inside, all the shelves and display cabinets were filled with crystals of all colours and shapes: some rough and some polished, some already in gift pouches and some in trays for you to choose your own. There were crystal gem trees and crystal bookends, key rings and wind chimes. The atmosphere was thick with incense and there was a strange thumping and wailing sound coming from the speaker in the corner. A CD cover propped up by the till informed them that they were listening to *Earth Healing – Shamanic Drumming*. Amy went over to look at a cabinet filled with jewellery and Zed headed for a table draped with tie-dye silk, on which stood a crystal ball, surrounded by boxes of wands, all carved out of different woods. A handwritten sign told you that you should not ignore the one you were initially drawn to; it was your friend and ally!

'Luke would love it in here,' said Amy, fingering a pack of tarot cards. 'He's really into exploring all this stuff – he calls it his dark side.'

'Does he have a light side?' said Zed, glancing at her sister, but instead of rushing to Luke's defence, Amy said, 'He reads loads of books on the spirit world and the paranormal and reckons he is naturally in tune with the dead.'

'Don't you think that's a bit weird?' said Zed, trying not to let it show that she knew it was very weird. And that he was. *Very weird!*

'What's weird about questioning the world around you? Thinking about what's here, apart from the obvious?'

Zed shrugged. 'It's just not very – cheerful?'

Amy wasn't impressed.

'Maybe he has nothing to be cheerful about. Maybe neither of us do! Has that ever occurred to you, Little Miss Sunshine?' she hissed.

The shopkeeper looked up from his book on meditation and Zed moved away from her sister to some ornately carved square boards.

But Amy followed her.

'He's got one of those, too,' she said. 'It's a Ouija board.'

'What's it for?' asked Zed.

'Talking to people on the other side.'

'The other side of what?'

'Dead people!'

'Yeah, right,' said Zed, but a quick look at her sister and she knew she wasn't joking.

Okay, this was really beginning to creep her out and the smell of the incense was making her feel sick. She wanted to go back out into the street and yet – and yet – she couldn't quite let this one go.

'Dead people? What, he's actually talked to dead people?'

'Yeah, with some of his friends. And I did it with them a couple of times too.'

'That is so freaky.'

'Well, that's what you *would* say, because you're nearly fourteen going on nine and so you're just not capable of getting it.'

'What's to get? You're all just doing it to spook yourselves out!'

Amy's eyes suddenly filled with tears.

'Maybe I just wanted to see if it was possible.'

Zed frowned, shook her head and picked up some Tibetan hand cymbals.

'Maybe,' said Amy, 'I thought if I could talk–'

But Zed didn't let her finish. 'You just did it because Luke did it.'

'Oh, don't start–'

'And it's freaky, not just *because it's freaky*, but because you did it *just* because he wanted you to, like that was enough.'

Amy narrowed her eyes.

'Ha – bring it on, Zed. The voice of experience, eh? Oh so goddam wise when, as far as I know, you've never even kissed a boy, let alone actually liked one, I mean properly liked. At your age I'd say that's freaky!'

Zed dropped the cymbals with a clang and walked out of the shop.

She marched back into the centre of town, past the harbour and on towards the castle up on the headland. She marched as fast as she could, without actually breaking into a run, trying to put as much distance as possible between her and Amy, and Mum and Dad too for that matter, and when the road started to gain height, she could feel her heart thumping in her chest.

She's right. She's right. She's right.

The houses got smarter and the view over towards the other side of the estuary got more and more spectacular, but Zed was not in the mood to be impressed. Her phone rang, it was Amy, and she thrust it deep into her pocket.

There was a sign with a picture of a parasol and a sandcastle, and an arrow pointing straight ahead, but after ten minutes, even at that pace and when Zed was feeling increasingly light-headed, there was still no evidence of the promised beach. She stopped, shut her eyes for a moment and gripped onto a lamp post to steady herself.

A jeep, done up to look like a train pulling three open-top carriages, chugged past her while a woman at the back pointed out things of interest with the help of a tinny megaphone.

And Dad thinks London Transport sucks.

She set off again and around the next corner the road narrowed and there were streaks of sand glistening on the tarmac.

She didn't see it coming. Or hear it. Just felt something strike the back of her head, a hard cuff shunting her forwards. She stumbled and fell face-first into the sand. And as she lay there with her eyes squeezed shut, before she noticed that her mouth was full of salty grit, instead of ice cream, and her fingers were sticky not with Cornish Vanilla, but her own blood, she wondered what the hell had happened – and then she saw it.

A bird. Standing still and erect on the back of a concrete bench, its hooked beak tilted open like a pair of secateurs.

A rush of heat rose up her throat to her face. Zed looked down at her hands. They were trembling; the smeared blood already dried, so it took a moment to work out which finger – or was it her head? No. There, on the pad of her thumb, a small hole, flooding dark red as she rubbed the skin.

The cormorant?

Zed sat up, spat out the sand and wiped her lips on her arm. She hadn't really wanted the ice cream anyway, not after the hot chocolate, but it had been a distraction, going to buy one from the van at the top of the beach, and she thought it might make her feel a bit better, at the very least cool her down.

She looked at the bird again.

If it had been a seagull, it would have pounced on the waffle cone lying in the sand and that would explain it, but this bird did nothing. It just glowered at her and twitched.

There weren't many people left now that the sun had gone behind the rocky headland. The surfers had swaggered up the beach, peeled off their wetsuits in the car park and driven off in their camper vans. The families with young kids had left, laden with wet towels, fishing nets, buckets and spades. A skinny girl in a teeny bikini was wrapped around her boyfriend, kissing his neck and giggling while he tried to read, but they obviously hadn't seen anything. They wouldn't notice Zed if she stripped off and started cartwheeling down the beach. No one would notice her. No one she wanted to notice. Not today. Not ever.

If it was the cormorant, what if it had properly hurt her? What if– *Get a grip.* What if– *Heart going too fast.*

What the hell was happening?

Take a deep breath Zed. And another. And another.

Four

As well as eggs and cheese, Cordelia sold flowers, made jam and took in sewing. Dad was delighted with his new neighbour, especially when she told him she had a yeast starter. He wouldn't stop banging on about it.

'She's been maintaining it for thirty years. Imagine that,' he said, rubbing his hands together. 'And she's going to give me half of it and keep us supplied with eggs, and in return I said I'd pop a loaf her way once in a while.'

Zed, still feeling grotty, replied with a very half-hearted, 'Whoop, whoop!'

'Don't knock it,' said Dad. 'Thirty-year-old yeast, that's pretty special.'

'You're telling me!'

But after a couple of days and still no sign of the actual freakin' yeast, Zed decided she'd have to get it herself, just to shut him up.

She'd never seen anything like Cordelia's kitchen. It was so full of stuff. There was a rusty oven and a big stone sink at one end and a little woodburning stove at the other, and crammed in between was a small dresser, a settle, numerous piles of logs and a fridge wedged under the stairs. In the middle of the room a mahogany table was completely covered in crockery, glasses, newspapers, bits of string, eggcups, jam jars and used stamps. The shelves were the same and suspended from the ceiling were wicker baskets, pans, bits of rope, a fishing rod, two driftwood mobiles and a pair of tights stuffed with wool. Everything was dusty and at first glance not that clean, but the over-all effect was cosy and warm.

'I've come for the yeast,' said Zed.

'Bottom shelf,' Cordelia pointed at the fridge. 'On the right.'

Zed picked up a Kilner jar with an orange seal, the contents looked white and pasty.

'Open it then!'

She did as she was told and took a sniff, trying to imagine how anything that had been festering away for that long was not going to kill them. It smelled strange, a bit like vinegar.

'It will make good bread, that,' said Cordelia with a huff, 'and I bet you won't be pulling that face when you're eating it!'

'I met your granddaughter.'

'What? Oh, you mean Tamsin! She's my great-granddaughter.'

'Does she go to Clewmor Academy then?' Zed was trying to keep her voice light and airy.

'Of course, where else would she go?'

'How – how old is she?'

'Fourteen, I think. What with all her studies and working in the shop, I don't see her very often, not anymore.'

Oh great. Same year. Same school.

On the top shelf of the dresser Zed noticed a limp, faded ragdoll. She was completely threadbare and even her one little leather button eye had lost its shine. What was left of her hair was stuffed into a cap, and her head flopped to one side. Zed went to prop her up but hesitated, not sure if it was okay to touch.

'Kerra made that for me,' said Cordelia. 'She was my nurse you see, before Gawen started wooing her with his mackerel and his sprats. My mother was always busy with my brothers and the farm work, so Kerra used to take me off her hands.'

'Kerra, from the boathouse?'

'Well, she wasn't really from the boathouse, but she spent most of her time down there because that was where Gawen lived. It was a proper little love nest. She never stopped talking about him, sighing, giggling, kissing me because I was the next best thing. And it was always *Gawen this, Gawen that.* She told me how one day he filled the boathouse with bluebells, every pot, cup, he'd even turned out the tin he used to store his fishing hooks. *The carpet of flowers was one thing, but using that tin,* she said, and she had that look, I'll never forget it, like she was wrapped up in silk and sunshine, *that speaks more of love than any of your fancy words.* She had it all planned out, what she was going to do when they got married. *The boathouse will do us just fine,* she'd say, *me, Gawen and a baban.* She'd have made a good mother.'

Cordelia stared down at her knotty brown hands.

'I often think of her. Even after all this time. Guess that's why Dicky Glynn gave me these bits and pieces.' She picked up an earthenware bowl and turned it over. 'Who'd have thought it, eh? They've been in the boathouse all this time.'

She filled the bowl from the milk jug, put it down by the back door and began humming.

'She used to sing me a lullaby, but I can't quite – I can't remember the tune. It's been driving me crazy. These last few weeks–'

'What happened to her?' asked Zed, but Cordelia didn't hear.

'—and the words – something about the song being in the rain and the woods and in their bones. She and Gawen were always singing in the evenings. They'd sit on the slip to catch the last of the light. He had a fiddle and he wasn't bad at all. If I could just get the opening...'

She screwed up her face in concentration while shoving the window open and calling the cats.

Zed picked up the Kilner jar and made her way to the door.

'Take a pot of jam while you're at it,' said Cordelia, pointing to a jar on the table. 'It might sweeten up your sister!'

It was gooseberry jam, dated last summer.

'Thank you,' said Zed.

The cats, all at once, threw themselves backwards, squealing, twisting and tripping over each other. Three ran straight under the table and the other one stood, feet planted wide, claws out, back arched and hissing. Its ears were twisted back and flat against his head.

'Polly?' Cordelia took a step towards her. 'Puss?'

The cat hissed again. Her fur was standing on end and her tail lashed from side to side.

'What on earth is the matter?' Cordelia whispered.

Polly took a small step towards the bowl then sprang back again, her eyes narrowed to thin slits. She shrank into the corner and began to yowl.

Cordelia used her foot to nudge the bowl towards the table legs. The cats who'd taken refuge there started spitting until one made a break for it, a streak of orange, screeching as it tore past Zed. It leaped up over the draining board and onto the window ledge before hurling itself out into the garden.

Zed lifted the jug and sniffed it.

'Nothing wrong with the milk,' she said.

Cordelia had slumped down on the settle, like the ragdoll on the shelf, and shut her eyes. Zed picked up the jam and tip-toed towards the door.

'I'm not asleep!'

'No, of course not,' said Zed, turning quickly.

'Only babies should sleep during the day!'

'Um – okay, well, I'll be going now anyway.'

Cordelia reached for the lip of the table and pulled herself upright.

'There were no babies for Kerra. And no more singing,' she said as she crossed the room, picked up a basket and started climbing the wooden stairs. When she reached the top step, she paused for a moment and called back down, 'She drowned, you see. Out in the harbour.'

Zed watched Cordelia's feet vanish onto the landing, then she turned back to the door, lifted the latch and let herself out.

That afternoon Mum sanded all the woodwork in the bathroom, Amy was sulking in her bedroom again, this time because Dad wouldn't drive her to the garage to buy cigarettes, and Zed wrote her postcards and put them in the post box in the wall at the end of the garden. She then made four origami butterflies and she tore all her packing paper into strips, found the wallpaper paste, blew up some balloons and started on her papier maché masks.

Dad was nowhere to be seen. Until suppertime, that is, when he arrived at the kitchen door beaming and holding up a loaf of delicious smelling, freshly baked bread.

Five

And that was the start of it. Over the next couple of weeks he made granary loaves and sourdough rolls, rye bread with cheddar cheese and walnut bread with rosemary and sea salt. They had bread for breakfast, lunch, supper and often in between. And it was all that Dad could talk about. In the morning, instead of helping Mum wash the windows or clearing out the gutters, he'd demonstrate different techniques for kneading and shaping dough. In the evenings when he could have hung up some pictures or ripped up the floral carpet on the stairs, he'd lecture anyone who'd listen on the superiority of wild over active dry yeast. The day he discovered you could put ice cubes in the oven to create steam, giving the bread a crispy crust, he leaped around the kitchen as if he'd won the lottery. Even Mum, who seemed to find his enthusiasm rather endearing to begin with, started to roll her eyes when he came bounding into the kitchen with his latest batch of bread and top tips for baking it. She continued to add to the list of jobs on the blackboard and then tick them off by herself, one by one.

A week passed. The landline had been connected, which meant Zed could actually call Beth and Caitlin without the slog up the hill, but even though both she and Amy had asked, nagged and even offered to do it themselves, there was still no sign of the internet. Amy was all for demanding an emergency family meeting, but their track record for progress, or even civility at these 'summits' was not encouraging. So Zed had a better idea. She drifted into the kitchen at suppertime and said, 'When are you going to make some saffron bread then?'

'Saffron?'

'Yeah, you know, the yellow stuff. I was reading about it, when I was out walking. It's a real Cornish thing and adds an amazing flavour and colour to breads and cakes and stuff. The Phoenicians brought it over when they came to trade tin.'

Mum nearly choked on her linseed crust.

'There are some super cool bread baking tutorials online,' she continued, as Mum and Dad exchanged astonished looks.

'There's this woman, right, who runs a lush artisan bakery. She's developed all her own recipes and has lots of ideas for like, using wood-fired ovens and adding weird stuff to yeast. She's got thousands of hits.'

Dad had just ripped up a tomato and basil twist and put it in a basket on the table.

'Sounds great, Zed! I'll look into it.'

Amy, who'd watched from the door, wandered in and poked the bread as if it might be alive and possibly dangerous. She licked her finger and nodded, slowly, which was about as much approval as anyone could hope for.

The following afternoon though, when Dad announced he was off to sort out the broadband, she was well impressed.

Zed found a list of boats for sale, some nice shiny inflatables and a big green plastic canoe, but Dad ignored them and bought a wooden boat from a man down in Clewmor.

'It's much more in keeping with the house,' he explained.

'Yeah, that figures,' Zed replied. 'It's knackered and it leaks!'

'Well ladies,' he announced after supper, 'I've got the bakery, the bread, the boathouse and the boat. It's time to lift this baby off the ground.'

Six

Dad wouldn't listen.

'It'll be fine!' he said, as he jogged up to the bakery after breakfast. The sky was the colour of the granite steps.

At lunch, when he popped back to make himself a coffee, Mum reminded him of the forecast. Even Cordelia, who didn't have access to a weather app, knew there was going to be a storm.

'The cats always hide down by the stove when a gale is on its way,' she said, pointing to the sky, 'and all four of them have been huddled up there since dawn!'

The air was heavy and still. The origami butterflies in Zed's room had ceased their gentle sway and hung static, frozen in mid-flight. The trees were completely still. The willows down by the stream looked artificial, like a painted backdrop. And as the afternoon progressed, the sky got darker, shade by shade, as if someone were working their way down the greys on a swatch card of paints.

But Dad was determined. He didn't want to wait any longer. He'd made a plan and wasn't going to let the weather get in the way. He'd arranged to take his bread into Clewmor, and he was aiming for late afternoon so that he could catch the deli and a couple of café owners at the quieter end of their working day. At the same time he'd call in at Clewmor Hall, before evening service began, and several B&Bs who thought they might like to up their game.

He brought a selection of rolls and loaves down from the bakery at half past three and wedged them in big straw baskets lined with gingham tea towels.

'I'll take them down to the boathouse,' he said. 'Zed will you help me?'

'No! I'm not going to encourage you,' she replied. 'It's insane.'

'Come on, I'll give you a cash bonus – when I get my first order.'

Mum shook her head and went back to sanding the banister on the landing.

It seemed odd to put on an anorak and wellies when it was so hot, but that's exactly what Zed did. She had a pretty good idea that Cordelia's cats knew better what was coming than her dad.

It was only a short walk down to the river, but her limbs felt sluggish and she couldn't find a comfortable way of moving with the basket. It hung off her elbow, thumped against her thigh with every step and she felt the dull ache of a bruise, long before she reached the boathouse.

As Dad fumbled with the keys, the first fat drop of rain landed on the top of her head. They paused to listen to a distant grumbling in the sky.

'Unbelievable,' said Dad.

'It really isn't,' replied Zed.

'Why today?' He seemed genuinely surprised.

'Why not today, Dad?'

He pushed open the side door and it dragged across the flagstones, leaving a series of chalky white marks. Together, as more raindrops slapped the backs of their necks, they bundled the three big baskets into the room and followed quickly, forcing the door shut behind them. Zed looked around. It was about as far from the romantic little cottage Cordelia had described as it was possible to get. It seemed dry, that was something, but the ceiling was low, and the three small windows let in very little light. At the far end of the room was an old stove on which sat two chipped mugs and an iron kettle. Above this was a mirror with spotted, metallic-looking glass. Two deck chairs were propped up against the wall beside a narrow metal camp bed with an old sagging mattress turned up on its side. That was it, apart from Dad's boat, the outboard engine and a set of oars, the varnish long since blistered and peeled away.

Zed shuddered.

The rumbling was closer now. Much closer. They looked at the bread, all wrapped up in lovely red and white cotton, and they looked at each other.

Suddenly the sky flashed. And the soft hiss of rain on the roof became louder, then the noise shifted to a drumming, then a pounding, and all the individual bullets of water blended into one great savage torrent of rain.

'Um, Dad,' Zed began, 'I don't think you're going to want to boat this lot down to Clewmor. Not now.'

There was no reply.

'It's filthy out there.'

'But I've spent all day baking!'

'Yeah, I get it Dad, but why not try and go down first thing in the morning?'

He grunted.

'I know it won't be quite as warm or quite as fresh but—'

'I could drive it in.'

'But if we carry it back up to the house, it will be sodden. Just leave it here overnight and come down when the storm has blown through. Then you can boat it in as planned.'

They stood for a moment, listening to the rain.

'I guess I don't really have a choice, do I?' said Dad, looking out of the window. His voice was small, like a disappointed child.

'Not really,' said Zed.

Know how that one feels...

The sky concurred with a boom of thunder, followed almost immediately with a jagged bolt of lightning.

And that's when Zed felt it. Like a punch.

Got to get out. Now.

Of course it made sense to wait in the dry, but even the howling wind and the vicious rain seemed a safer option than staying inside, where she really didn't want to be and a sitting target for – *for what?*

'Let's go!' she yelled.

'It's okay Zed, we'll just wait for a few minutes.'

'No! No, it's not.' She surprised herself by the panic in her voice.

'Alright, well, let's get–'

But she was already out of the door, running through the puddles and flying clods of sodden leaves. The sky cracked again, lighting up the heavens with a Harry Potter scar. And the rain – it was merciless; cutting into her scalp as her hood was yanked back by the wind, but she didn't care – she didn't care as long as she was moving! Moving away from the boathouse.

'Nearly there, nearly there,' she gasped as she slipped and stumbled along the path. She paused for a moment under the viaduct, to peel her hair off her face, then she set off again at a sprint, and did her best to keep up that pace all the way back to the house. She ran panting and pasted with wet leaves into the kitchen, and threw herself at the Aga.

'Well?' said Mum. 'Shall I run a bath?'

Zed grabbed her and clung to her shoulders.

'Hey – hey,' said Mum. 'What's up, pet? Where's Dad? Is he okay?'

'I'm scared!' whispered Zed, pressing her face into Mum's dry hair.

'Shh – hey – it's a proper squall like, I'll give you that, but there's no need for tears.'

Zed took a deep breath and loosened her grip.

She hadn't even known she was crying.

Seven

In the morning the sun was shining, and the sky was clear. It would have been hard to recall the ferocity of the storm had it not been for the moss-covered branches strewn all over the lawn, and a large bit of guttering lying in a puddle on the gravel. When Zed got downstairs Dad was pacing up and down the kitchen.

'Maybe I should just start over.'

'Stop being such a divvy,' said Mum. 'Go and get them and then at least you'll know if they're edible.'

Dad nodded. 'You coming, Zed?'

'No,' she said quickly. 'I'm going to check on Cordelia.'

'What a night, my girl! Over here. Give me a moment...' Cordelia was making her way slowly down from the field above her cottage. She was wearing what looked like big black waterproof fishing trousers, but on closer inspection proved to be bin liners held together with duct tape.

'Just checking you survived the storm!' said Zed.

'Humph – I got off lightly. The caravan will be sodden inside of course, one of my hen houses turned over and the tarpaulin has gone from the top of the goats' shed, but that's it.'

'Can I help at all?'

'I might need you and your sister.'

Amy didn't tend to get up unless she had to. Amy didn't tend to be helpful, unless she had to. And then it was usually accompanied with such a surplus of eye rolling, groaning and scowling, that it felt as far from a generous gesture as it was possible to get. So when Zed knocked nervously on her sister's door and explained why Amy was needed, she was almost lost for words when she heard, 'Sure, come in', through the keyhole.

'Wasn't that sick?' said Amy, grinning. She was sitting crossed-legged on her bed in one of Luke's old long-sleeved t-shirts. 'I sat up all night, listening to it.'

Zed looked around, amazed.

'Oh yeah, I – you know, sorted some stuff.'

She hadn't moved in exactly, her boxes were still piled up by the door where they'd been left by the removal men, but she'd unpacked one suitcase the contents of which – posters, postcards, photos, and her collection of old record sleeves, covered the entire wall above her bed. There were letters and drawings, tarot cards and a couple of band t-shirts pinned to her headboard too, and three small purple cushions propped up on her pillow.

'It looks great in here.'

'Yeah, well,' the scowl was back. 'Needs must.'

'My great-grandson used to help me with things like that,' said Cordelia, watching the girls drag the large piece of tarpaulin out of the brambles and secure it back on the roof of the goats' shed with some big hunks of rock.

'Where's he now then?' asked Zed.

'Playing silly beggars. Come on in and I'll poach you an egg.'

When Zed got back, Dad was still sitting at the kitchen table, waiting for his boots to dry.

'Come on Shaun,' said Mum, 'just go down and see what's what. Sitting here staring at your socks isn't going to achieve anything, is it?'

Dad muttered something.

'You'll go with him, won't you Zed?'

'I've got to–' This time her mind went blank.

'Please, Zed.' Mum gave her that stare.

'But – I don't want to!' she replied.

'Why not?'

'Because–' Zed looked out of the window, at the blue sky and little puffy clouds and she really couldn't think of an excuse. Not one that made any sense, anyway.

The boathouse had taken quite a battering. Bits of slate had been wrenched off the roof and were lying half-submerged in the water. The side door had blown open and a huge branch coated in white fungus was wedged up against it. Inside, the rain had pooled in a swampy puddle in the middle of the floor. The bread seemed okay though. Maybe it was all the moisture in the air, but once Zed had removed a few damp leaves and twigs from the baskets, Dad tore open a couple of loaves to find them still soft and springy and smelling delicious. It was enough to convince him that he was back on track.

The tide was low, but there was a clear channel from the boathouse out to the deeper water and once he'd rolled up his trousers and dragged the boat down the granite slipway, Dad clamped the outboard engine onto the transom and lifted in his precious cargo. It took three sharp tugs on the cord and then he was off, chugging out into the middle of the river. Zed waved and turned, eager to get back to the house. And that's when she saw them: four bashed up, bloody black feathers, lying by the side of the slip.

Eight

Mum and Dad were having a row. A full-on, almighty humdinger of a row. And it was bad. Just like the old days. Before the days when Mum had stopped caring, which were worse, and before the *worst* day when she'd almost given up for good.

Zed came into the kitchen to find Amy hunched up on the floor by the Aga, all elbows and knees, Mum draped over the table with her head in her hands and Dad pacing up and down, whinging about some man in Clewmor. Dad had taken his samples all over town apparently, everyone was keen to try them and nearly everyone had been very complimentary, but all he could focus on was this one man from a B&B next to the church, who had said Dad's rolls were *too chewy*.

'He's welcome to his bland, marshmallowy, stick-in-the-roof-of-your-mouth, nutritionally pointless, shouldn't-really-be-called-bread!'

'Let it go,' said Mum.

'And he can stuff it where the sun don't shine.'

Dad yanked open the door of the Aga, took out two rolls and slammed them onto the table.

'That's all that's left,' he said in a grumpy but apologetic voice. Like someone was going to be devastated not to get a bit of his two-day-old bread.

'Well then,' said Zed, trying to keep things upbeat, 'what's your problem? Considering you nearly had to abandon the whole batch.'

He gave one to Mum with a slab of butter so thick it looked like cheddar cheese. She waved it at Zed and Amy, who both shook their heads, then she removed half of the yellow brick and flicked it in the bin. Dad pretended not to notice, tore open the other one and stuffed a great hunk of it into his mouth.

'He obviously has no idea what bread can taste like!' he said through the chewing.

'Get over yourself,' Amy groaned.

Dad's eyes expanded and then narrowed ominously.

'Perhaps the fella's right,' said Mum quickly, taking a bite and chewing theatrically. 'Forget this poncey bread, let's go down the Asda for some proper scran!'

Zed and Amy giggled as they always did when Mum talked like Nanny Pam, but Dad didn't find it funny.

He started crashing around the kitchen banging utensils and throwing bowls and mugs into the sink.

'Stop being such an arse,' Amy yelled over the noise.

'Language!' Dad yelled back.

'Sense of humour malfunction!' Mum yelled even louder. She sounded exasperated, but the corners of her mouth were twitching.

Dad grabbed the sink with both hands. He waited for a moment before saying very slowly, through gritted teeth, 'I'd actually like your support on this, Lucy.'

All the humour drained from Mum's eyes. She replied quietly but very firmly,

'And what do you think the last couple of weeks has been all about? I have been painting and cleaning and sanding and sorting out the plumbing and the electrician and the house insurance – and what have you been doing? Fiddling about up in your precious bakery!'

Amy let out a long low whistle.

'And I'm absolutely bloody knackered! And bloody frustrated, because even though everything is meant to have changed, I'm still the one dealing with all the scutwork. You might not be away, not off at a conference somewhere, but you're still away in your own little world, oblivious to the rest of us!'

'Go girl!' yelped Amy. This was not helpful, but Mum was on a roll anyway. 'And even though this is what I feel and have felt all week, actually all last week too, I have tasted every bloody loaf that you've skipped down here to show off. I've eaten every bloody butty you've waved at me even when it was filled with beetroot bloody hummus! So don't you dare come back at me with *lack of support!*'

Dad turned. He seemed genuinely astonished.

'I've sorted out your workshop for you!' he said.

'Yep, that's true!' said Zed, looking anxiously back and forward between the two of them.

'Yes, but when the hell am I supposed to get up there?'

'Whenever you like,' he replied sulkily.

'No Shaun, because it's not just about us, is it? What about the girls? I'm trying to make a home for them. To make this a bit easier–'

'Well, that's an epic fail,' said Amy.

'So am I!' said Dad.

'No, you're just following some pipe dream and expecting us to fall in behind you.'

'It's your dream too. You're the one with all the memories of idyllic Cornish holidays. You're the reason we came here.'

'Really? I think we came here because you felt guilty. Guilty for all the times you weren't there. Guilty because you weren't there for me, when I really needed you to be, and you weren't there for Amy.'

Zed wrapped her arms around her belly and started squeezing as tight as she could.

'And you think that by choosing somewhere where I have a history rather than you, that this somehow redresses the balance?'

'Of course it does,' said Amy, oozing sarcasm. 'Yay! The perfect quick fix! Instant Happy Families.'

'Ha – we're *The Bakers*! Mr and Mrs Bun and the two Miss Buns!' Zed knew it was feeble as she said it. *Very feeble, but worth a try.*

Amy gave her a withering look, got up from the floor and left the room.

Dad stood at the sink staring out into the garden. Mum, who'd gone very pale, lowered her head back into her arms on the table and lay there, unnaturally still. Then she got up and slowly walked across to the fridge, opened it and uncorked a bottle of wine.

Nine

Cordelia had told Zed that there was a route into Clewmor via the woods. She said she hadn't done it in a while, but couldn't see why it wouldn't be possible to go by bike, as long a Zed was prepared to lift it over the stile. Zed was prepared to do almost anything to get out of Tremelin, to see some people, cars and pavements. There might not be many clothes buying opportunities, at least for those with any taste, but surely it wasn't too soon to send another batch of postcards?

Dad was sitting in the car by himself, staring out over the trees. When she told him where she was going, he nodded, even though she knew he hadn't really been listening.

'And I'll be buying three Pot Noodles for tea!' she called back as she walked to the gate.

Actually, that isn't such a bad idea...

At the viaduct, Zed took the right-hand branch of the track. It was steep and muddy after the storm, making cycling impossible. She trudged onwards though, anything to avoid the awful, familiar silence at home.

Cordelia had told her there was a stile at the top of the hill, above the bend in the river, where the two wind turbines came into view on the far side of the estuary, but she couldn't see them. She was able to get back on her bike as the path flattened out, but it was hard work cycling in the cloggy earth. Kab would say it was good for his quads.

She lifted up off the seat to see if she could see over the hedge, hit something and bounced over the handlebars into a clump of brambles.

Zed swore. Loudly. And boy did it feel good. She swore some more, really shouting this time, bellowing every piece of bad language she could think of. And she could think of quite a lot.

She looked at the cuts on her palms and wrists; thin red slices, they didn't really hurt, it was like they'd been drawn on in red Biro. Then she turned her attention to her bike. The mudguard was hanging off, she gave it a tug and it came away in her hand, and the front wheel had buckled into a boomerang shape, with snapped wonky spokes sticking out at funny angles. She pulled the bike upright. Although it bumped and lurched, if she pushed it, the wheel could still rotate, just.

She vaguely remembered seeing a cycle shop in Clewmor, somewhere down in one of the little streets leading onto the quay. In a few moments the stile came into view and then it was downhill most of the way.

The man in the shop looked at the wheel and scratched his head. Then he looked at Zed and grinned.

'Alright Miss? You think I be some kind a miracle worker?'

'Well, I–'

'Let's have a look, Dad.' Zed turned and the first thing she saw was a pair of long brown legs astride an overturned bike. Hang on – she'd seen those shoes before and those very short shorts, a different tight t-shirt, this time grey with the shop logo in neon orange, but it was definitely her. Zed braced herself.

'Holy Moly,' Tamsin whistled when she saw the front wheel. She came over, crossed her arms and leaned against the till. 'How d'you manage that then?'

'I hit a rock.'

'Oops,' she said and sniggered. 'Where?'

'Tremelin Woods.'

'Proper cross-country stuff! Not really the bike for it though, is it? What were you doing there?'

'I was told it was the quickest way to get down here, by your grandmother!'

'Great-grandmother, actually.'

'Yeah, okay. Whatever.'

Tamsin nodded, but didn't move. She was just warming up, though. Zed could sense it.

'No bikes lanes, eh?'

'What?'

'An' the signage is lousy.'

'I don't–'

'Never mind. Have you oiled it recently?'

Zed sighed.

'Or checked the brakes?'

She really didn't need this. It was a long walk home.

The man frowned at Tamsin and then said to Zed, 'Go on, leave it by the door then an' I'll do it dreckly.'

'Um, what, maybe, like an hour?'

He chuckled, just like his daughter.

'I'm good, but not *that* good. Better borrow one of ours.'

'I'm happy to walk–'

'You could do with some knee pads,' said Tamsin.

Here we go...

'An' you *definitely* need a helmet.'

'What's up with ev'ryone today, then?' said Tamsin's dad, shaking his head. He was on his knees fiddling with an inner tube while Tamsin pumped up the tyres of a hire bike. 'You not be the first to 'ave 'ad 'an accident. There was a nasty crash up by the sailing club first thing. Cuts an' bruises an' I don't know what. That bike's not for savin'.'

'And Tristo wobbled his off the town quay last night,' said Tamsin. She brushed her hair off her face leaving an oily smear on her forehead.

Why hasn't she got spots then? It's so unfair.

'That would be the drink!'

Unless all this fresh air is going to give me flawless, perfect skin too...

'I doubt it, Dad. He's got pissed in The Lugger every night for years an' it's the first time he's fallen into the harbour. Lucky for him, it was high tide!'

Wait. Was that a wink?

Tamsin gave the bike a shove so that it rolled across the shop floor. Zed caught it clumsily by the handlebars and when she looked up Tamsin was smirking at her. It made her feel about six.

A woman ran into the shop. She was puffing and grunting and stood for a moment with her hands on her knees before straightening up. When she pushed back her thick yellow hair, the face underneath was red and clammy. She could hardly get her words out.

'Bill? Bill, have you heard?'

'Slow down Doreen, take your time–'

'Heard what?' said Tamsin.

'It's the ferry. The Penkerris Ferry. It's gone out to sea. Straight out of the harbour–'

'What's the Penkerris Ferry?' asked Zed.

'Penkerris is the village on the other side of the estuary,' said Tamsin. 'The passenger ferry goes back an' forth all day. In the summer it keeps on going 'til the pubs shut.'

'Nice little earner,' said Bill.

'The point is,' said Doreen with her hands on her hips, 'it's not going back and forth now, it's heading for France!'

Tamsin and her dad looked at each other. Bill put down his tools and they hurried out into the street. Doreen bustled out after them and Zed followed. All the shopkeepers, their customers and anyone else who might have been passing were talking in little clusters, swaying on tiptoes, straining their necks and looking down towards the town quay. Bill scribbled a note and stuck it on the window then pulled out a bunch of keys and locked the door. By the time they reached the harbour steps, quite a crowd had gathered. One or two men were marching around, laughing and chatting, as if it was some kind of practical joke, but others spoke in hushed tones.

'They can't contact 'em by radio,' someone said.

'Well, the harbour master is on 'is way out there,' said someone else.

'What about the lifeboat?'

'What about fuel?'

'Who's on today?'

'Young Pete was doin' the first shift this morning. Dunno if they'd swapped yet.'

'What's 'ee playing at then?'

'What's 'ee thinking?'

'Do you reckon someone else 'as taken over? Like a hi-jackin'?'

'On the Penkerris Ferry? Who do you reckon they've got on there then, David Beckham?'

Suddenly the big orange lifeboat came into view and everyone went quiet, watching it glide past the quay. As soon as it reached the mouth of the harbour, the boat rose up in the water and sped off after the ferry.

'No point hanging around,' said Tamsin. 'They'll be a while.'

Zed ambled around town and watched as most people drifted back to work or took the opportunity to grab an early lunch, but an hour later there were still little huddles of people shaking their heads and talking in low voices. She sidled up to three women standing outside the butchers and listened to their conversation while pretending to read a fascinating poster about different cuts of beef.

'Gone to hospital for a check-up, is what I heard,' said one.

'Didn't know what came over hisself. Apparently 'ee doesn't remember anythin' since breakfast,' said another.

'Dear of 'im,' said the first, shaking her head and many chins.

'Dear of him? He could have killed all sixteen of them!'

'Wouldn't be good for business—'

'Depends on the business, doesn't it?' said the one who hadn't spoken yet. 'Old Frank Churcham would do well out of it!'

The first two looked at her and then started cackling. One of them swung her lumpy bag and whacked the one who'd just spoken on the arm.

'I'm thinkin' about ice cream parlours not funeral parlours, you old bat!'
They waved at each other, still chuckling, and set off in different directions.

It was too hot to cycle uphill and Zed pushed the hire bike most of the way home. When she reached Tremelin, Zed saw Cordelia leaning against her gatepost and talking to a pair of ramblers who were sitting on the grass outside her cottage and taking it in turns to drink from a thermos.

'Zed has been into Clewmor this afternoon, haven't you?' said Cordelia.

'Did you go up by the school?'

'No, I–'

'You didn't see what happened then?'

'No, but the lifeboat–' Zed began.

'No, up at the school,' said the man, eager to share the news. 'Someone was up on the roof and threatening to jump!'

'A science teacher,' said the woman. 'That's what they told us in the library. And the chap in the post office said he'd taught his daughter.'

'Very out of character,' said the man, slurping his drink. 'One minute he was full of beans, having breakfast with his wife, planning to pop into town to do a bit of shopping and the next–'

'You know him, then?' said Cordelia sharply. 'Know him well? Well enough to be able to comment on what is or isn't out of character?'

'We're only passing on what the librarian said,' said the woman, all wide-eyed and sweetness itself. 'We thought you'd want to know.'

They stood, picked up their sticks and clattered off up the lane.

'Gossip!' said Cordelia. 'Can't abide it.'

'Is it true though?' asked Zed, a little annoyed she hadn't taken the main road out of town. It was her school after all, or would be soon enough.

'I expect so,' said Cordelia, 'but I doubt that it's out of character. Something will have just unearthed that part of his character, a part that he chooses to keep hidden. Poor man.'

Buttons was snuffling about, eating biscuit crumbs left in the grass.

'I heard about the ferry,' she said. 'Most odd.' She shuffled towards her back door. 'And the fish and chip shop has shut, apparently. Decided last night, mid-season, when he does his best business and always has done! Because, he says, it struck him all of a sudden, that he never wants to see another fish!' She turned back and looked at Zed. 'Yes, it's most odd, most odd indeed.'

Ten

Tremelin Woods were best explored on foot. That much Zed had learnt and every day for the next week she took herself off there after lunch. She was amazed that no one seemed to mind her wandering around by herself, or even notice how long she was gone. In London, if she'd gone off on her bike, she'd have had to tell Mum where she was going and what time she'd be back. Certain routes were not permitted, especially if they involved a main road or the Hillfield Estate or worse, the corner of Markham Road where Luke's acne-scarred older brother used to hang out with his mates outside the boarded-up betting shop. Here, she could be gone for hours at a time and no one seemed to care.

Amy had barely left her room and Mum had stopped doing anything much. She said she'd exhausted herself and needed a few days to re-charge her batteries, but Zed had a bad feeling. Dad was still hanging around his bakery, but the rich, yeasty smells had been replaced for two days by a bitter aroma of burnt toast, followed by a day of thick sappy smoke wafting out over the garden, and now nothing. No chat, no smells, no bread!

The path that ran parallel to the river was dry and dusty where it twisted around the gnarled roots of the big oak trees. The tide was low and as she looked down to the left, Zed could see the boggy bank give way to grey-green mud and then a ridge of sand, glistening in the sun. She made several attempts to get down there, but each time became entangled in thick brambles until rounding another tree, she nudged her hips against the nettles, pushing them to the side, and managed to pick her way across the springy tufts of grass to the water's edge.

'Sshh... keep still!'

Zed swung around to see a scruffy looking boy, maybe sixteen or seventeen, with dark hair scraped into ponytail and a wispy beard. He was sitting on an upturned plastic crate, holding a sketchbook and had a pile of little lumps of charcoal by his feet.

'Bollocks, it's g–g–gone–'

Zed turned back towards the water, just in time to see a large black bird take off from the sand bank.

'I'm so sorry–' Zed began.

'Sshh...sh...shut up, will you?' The boy was holding his fists up towards his face, jerked a finger to his lips and pointed at another bird, a bit further along the bank. Zed watched it untuck its neck and raise itself up through an 'S' bend to form one almost straight line from yellow beak to glossy black tail. Then, with a little shudder, its wings unfolded and started to pulse: huge black wings with three layers of feathers, the bottom ones spreading out like a fan. And it was off too, raising itself vertically before flattening out and beating its way across the river. One long black wing angled down to the water, where with every stroke it seemed to brush its grainy reflection.

The boy turned back towards her, his eyes full of fury. Zed took a step backwards as he tugged his beard twice and then stood, drew his shoulders up, lifted his elbows behind him and shook his arms out. She wanted to get back up to the path, but the way he was moving was so bizarre that she had to stop and watch. It was a bit like the Tai Chi they'd done at school to celebrate the Chinese New Year. He lifted one arm and then the other and gently they began to throb, a slow, deep throb that included his neck and torso. He bent one way and then the other before straightening up, bringing his elbows back in line with his body and sitting down, but with his spine rigid and his chest pushed forward. He stared out at the water and gradually his body softened.

'I didn't mean to disturb you,' said Zed, nervously.

The boy grunted.

'Were you drawing it?'

'Wass it look like?' he hissed through gritted teeth. She waited a moment before his jaw relaxed.

'It's a cormorant, isn't it?'

He slammed his sketchbook shut, tugged on his beard again, dipped his head and started muttering under his breath.

Okay, time to get out of here.

But then the boy inhaled deeply and held out the book.

'Sorry!' he said, so fast that it sounded like a whistle. He flicked her a sideways glance.

'Of course it's a cormorant! 'Ave a look if you like. Lots of 'em down 'ere and now you've shown up,' he sighed heavily, 'them two won't be back for a bit.'

Zed hesitated, then stepped towards him. He brandished the book, and she took it.

'I watch 'em all day. Standin' like that, with their wings outstretched.'

'I see,' said Zed, who couldn't think of anything better to say. She was pretty convinced that sticking around wasn't such a great idea.

'Such 'ansome birds. You get lots down 'ere, of course. Egrets, redshanks, oystercatchers an' I sketch 'em too b-b-but none are as splendid as the cormorant. Look – there's another.'

And there was, indeed, another bird standing on a bit of driftwood, not far from where the first two had taken off. Its body was so sleek it looked like it had been painted in jet black oil, with a sheen of metallic purple or green, depending on the way the light fell when it twisted his head. Its eye was definitely green though, a shiny emerald bead.

Zed watched the boy lean forward in his seat, elongate his neck, and rotate his head towards her,

'Name means *raven of the sea*,' he said, 'an' my name's Denzil.' He wiped his hand down the front of his shirt and held it out to Zed, half raising himself awkwardly from his low seat. Zed hesitated then stepped closer, leaned in and shook it briefly.

'We've been around since the dinosaurs–' he spoke in a scratchy voice now and used his fingers to lift his eyelids so that he stared at her without blinking, his green eyes uncannily like the bird's. 'You'll find us all over. Wherever there be fish, salt water or fresh, no matter, in sea, river or lake, there's bound to be some kind of cormorant. We don't venture far away from the shore, mind.' Then suddenly he snapped out of it. 'Look, it's d–drying itself.' He pointed at the cormorant. It seemed to tremble for a moment and then spread out its wings.

'It's a bit like a pelican,' said Zed.

'Folks say they be related,' he replied. 'I'm guessin' it's the big bill.'

Then off he went, speaking really fast and every now and again jabbing the air with his finger. 'Folks 'ave a lot to say 'bout these birds, always 'ave. They're supposed to s...s...signify nobility, and good luck especially when there be three flyin' together, but more often they get a bad press. And I know what that feels like! It's why I like 'em.'

'What do you mean, bad press?'

'How long have you got?' But he didn't wait for an answer. 'Okay, let's start with the B–B–Bible. They're mentioned four times in the Old Testament: Leviticus, D–Deuteronomy, Isaiah, Zephaniah and each time they're ranked with the unclean. Yep, I know what that feels like too!' he said, sniffing at his armpit.

Zed laughed.

'Then Sh...Sh...Shakespeare uses the word *cormorant* as a synonym for *voracious*!'

'Ah,' said Zed.

He looked at her and rolled his eyes.

'It means greedy.'

'Yeah, I knew that,' she said, a bit too quickly.

'Well, takes one to know one, I guess, but we're *much* greedier than them. So much greedier. And it's not just Sh...Shakespeare who's at it. In *Paradise Lost*, M...M...Milton says S...S...Satan breaks into Paradise and sits on the tree of life, *like a cormorant, devising death, to them that lived*. Well, you can't get much more damning than that, can you?'

'No, I guess not.'

So, like I say, a b-bad press.'

'Maybe it's because they look so creepy.'

His eyes narrowed, he dipped his head again and his hands balled up, but he shook them out almost immediately, tugged his beard and said, 'Others get it, though. In s...stories. That there's more to them, I mean. You go to school, right?'

'Yeah, obviously.'

'Well, when I did, which wasn't very often, so actually it's not obvious smartarse, we did Greek mythology. An' that was actually quite cool. I managed three days on the trot when we did the *O-Odyssey*. Did you do that?'

'Maybe,' said Zed, who had vague memories of a primary school teacher bringing in a donkey piñata to illustrate the story of the Trojan horse.

'Then you'll remember the sea nymph, disguisin' 'erself as a cormorant an' helping Odysseus stay afloat after a storm?'

Nah. Not ringing any bells.

'Well, that sounds a bit more, um, helpful,' said Zed.

'Well, that's just it. They can be helpful if you know how to engage with 'em. An' it's not just the Greeks that knew that, it's the Chinese, the Polynesians and there be loads of stuff in Norwegian folklore too.'

Zed was still thinking about Beth smashing up the donkey and giving her all the jelly beans because they were her favourite.

'An' yeah, you don't want 'em as your enemy. If you're s...s...set against them, you're screwed, but all the s...stories of messages from the dead an' the like, it depends how you take it, doesn't it?'

Zed nodded. 'Right, well, I'd better be going–'

'In Ireland, they say one s...s...sitting on a church st-steeple is a warning that there's danger ahead, but I'd rather know, wouldn't you? Iss *help*ful, like you say, you can prepare! An' there are lots of stories about bringing fisherman luck.'

'Yep, well–'

'An' is true, you know. A f...fisherman from Oslo, who used to work down

Newlyn way, once told me 'is people knew those who died at s...s...sea visited their old homes in the form of a cormorant! An' he wasn't just talking stories, his best friend died out on the lifeboat an' he saw him every day sitting on a b-b-buoy in the harbour, lookin' out for them all.'

'I'm going to head off now.'

'Oh, they be intelligent birds all right; adaptable, an' they don't forget. Them birds don't forget a thing.'

Something shifted in his eyes, the shoulders hunched up again, the elbows pushed out behind, the hands splayed and then he was back – all human. Just a boy talking to a girl in a wood.

'Where you be from then?' he asked turning to face her for the first time.

'We've just moved into Tremelin House.'

He grunted. 'Don't go that way meself, not these days.'

Zed realised she was still holding his sketchbook. 'Can I see your drawings?'

'Gave 'em to you, didn't I?' He shrunk into his coat and yanked his beard.

There was nowhere for her to sit, so wedging her foot against a tree trunk, she leaned the book on her thigh, opened it carefully and turned over the pages, one by one.

'Those are herons, just up from here. An' that's the yellow flag iris,' said Denzil. 'You'd 'ave seen that I s'pose. Ah, but not the b-bluebells, they were out in May. And you've missed the wild garlic, the whole woods stank of it! Wonderful to eat mind, I picked sacks of the stuff. Ah, there you go. The cormorants...'

And there were pages and pages of them; a few in pencil, but mainly charcoal. Some were just simple two or three lines capturing the bird in flight, the soft curves of its breast and neck, and others were more detailed. And then there was writing too, little hunched up, spiky words, with sketches all over the margins, jabbing and swooping round the text.

'See – I've written down some of the stories too!' he pointed.

Zed turned to a couple of watercolours, loosely inserted into the book. The first was of a nest with three pale blue eggs and the next was all about the splash: the frothy whites and dabs of blue sitting above the sleek black torpedo of the bird, easing its way through the water.

'Do they dive for fish then?' she asked.

'They don't dive, you t-t-tuss, they swim! In fact, we can swim better than a fish,' he said proudly, and he was up on his feet, his arms above his head, hands pressed together like an arrow. 'We can dive down, I'll give you that, a long, long way, but we use our wings an' feet, to chase an' twist an' turn. That's swimmin' in my book. An' it's as elegant as a ballerina.'

He stopped abruptly and looked at Zed, slouching in her jeans and her trainers. 'Don't s'pose you be a dancer then?'

She stood up straight. 'I could if I–'

But he didn't let her finish.

'It's hard to catch a likeness when they're movin', but most often, if they're not disturbed,' he said, pointedly, 'they're still enough!'

'I said I was sorry.'

'Mind you, the other night they were actin' so teasy!' He hopped from one foot to the other, twisting his body as if he was in pain. 'D'you remember, the night when it was pizen down? They was screeching an' squawking an' pecking at each other. Leaving feathers all over the path. Actually drawing blood! Like somethin' 'ad addled their brains!' he said, frowning.

'I can believe it!' said Zed, who found his re-enactment unsettling enough.

'I left 'em to it. I often sleep 'ere, under the st-stars, away from people and all their c-c-crap, but not that night.'

Zed had reached the end of the drawings and she shut the book.

'They're very good,' she said, handing it back. He took it with a nod.

'I like drawing. And it likes me. It k-k-keeps me from – I did nearly do a whole year of classes in Falmouth, at the Art School – but then, you know, they wanted stuff, p-p-portfolios, artist's statement an' all that. When people want stuff from me, that's when I'm outta there–'

'Seems a shame,' said Zed.

'Yeah, well, maybe you'll see some of these in Tremarrak Library, next year – I go there to use the computer an' that an' the woman there loves b-b-birds too. She suggested a little exhibition, like, on my own terms, when I want, no need to sweat it.'

'I hope you do!'

Denzil grinned. 'I might s...s...sell one or two, then them birds will pay for us dinner! Oh, listen now – it's callin'.'

A tremor shuddered up the cormorant's neck. It tucked its head back, stretched its beak open in a yawn, and out came a belching sort of squawk. It was such an odd and unexpected sound that Zed had to stifle a giggle.

'It sounds like someone twisting a balloon,' she said. 'Really slowly.'

Denzil threw back his head and laughed. Then he dipped his chin, lifted his head and squawked too.

'Well, I'll be leaving you both to your – friends,' she said.

'Friends. Yeah. I like that,' he said, still grinning.

Zed started walking back towards the woods.

'Mind you, cormorants an' humans 'aven't always been friends,' Denzil called after her, 'b-b-backalong we treated them somethin' rotten. Every now an' then some stupid idiot got an idea in his 'ead that they were interferin' with the fishermans' catch. Then they'd 'ave a cull. A big one.'

'What, they'd kill them?' said Zed, twisting around.

'Too right. In 1911 them know-it-alls up at County Hall offered one sh… shillin' for ev'ry head of a cormorant or sh…shag an' that went on 'til ten thousand dead birds 'ad been 'anded over! T-t-ten thousand bloody birds. Literally! B-but when they got round to lookin' in their stomachs, there were lots of sand eels an' the like, but not that much those fisherman might 'ave sold in the market. Not enough for them to threaten anyone's livin'!'

'Mmm – I could understand if they didn't want to be friends after that,' said Zed.

'Zactly!' Denzil replied with a nod. He leaned over and picked up a lump of charcoal and then opened the book on his lap, 'See you then–'

'It's Zed.'

'Zed,' he said, without looking up again. 'Right on.'

Zed turned towards the trees again. The crushed, sodden grass still marked her route down to the riverbank, so she took the same steps in reverse and found her way back to the path.

Eleven

Amy was sitting on the floor in the kitchen, red-eyed and picking at her fingernails.

'I hate him. I hate him. I hate him.' She was chanting through gritted teeth.

'What happened?'

'Where the hell is Mum?' Amy asked, looking accusingly at Zed.

'I don't know. What's been going on?'

'Dad told me to sort out my head. That's a joke, right? Coming from him? Like, he's got it all worked out? He said I had to stop calling Luke, because it was *his* fault I was such a mess. And it was *his* fault that this family was falling apart.'

'He's a bit stressed–'

'We're the ones that should be stressed with his Mr Psycho-Looney Baker routine. I mean, what's that all about? He keeps telling me I'm screwing up my life, but thinks eating a bread roll will make all the difference. It's insane!'

'He's trying to–'

'Why are you defending him? He's the one that's screwed up our lives. Not me. Not Luke. When he pissed off and left us with Mum. When she should've been put away–'

'She was depressed, not mad.'

'Well running away didn't help, did it?' Amy screamed at Zed.

'Why are you shouting at me? It's not my fault!' said Zed.

'No, nothing is ever your fault.'

'Yet I'm still being punished!' Zed screamed back. 'And I've still been dragged here too, haven't I? You know, you're not the only one who's been separated from someone they care about. And none of this is for my benefit, but I've just got to go along with it, 'cause apparently, it's the best thing for everyone else!'

Amy stared at her.

'So I'm trying my best here. I really am trying to keep an open mind and give it a go, but if you could all stop for one minute and see things from my point of view, you would understand that *if* we're going to play the blame game, then I should be the one doing most of the blaming!'

'Whatever–' said Amy in her most withering voice.

And that did it. Zed felt something explode inside her. She needed something, something to– She looked at the wine glass in the sink, but then picked up a jug from the draining board and hurled it, as hard as she could, at the wall. It bounced off, and fell, smashing onto the slate. The sound was glorious.

They stared at the thick shards of pottery, quivering on the floor.

'What the–? Was that aimed for me?' Amy whispered, her face crumpled and she started to cry.

'Not exactly–'

Zed knelt down and put her arms around her sister. She expected to be shrugged off at the very least, quite possibly punched, but instead Amy leaned against her for a bit and then crawled out into the middle of the floor and started picking up the remains of the jug.

There was a newspaper lying on the table and she opened it out and began to wrap the pieces of pottery. A few layers down she paused to read, raised an eyebrow and the corners of her mouth and held up the page to Zed. There was a large colour photograph under the headline, *Calm after the Storm*.

Zed recognised the church in Clewmor, against a backdrop of blue sky. She nodded, tried to smile, then squinted and moved closer. It was hard to tell, there were trees in the way and the image was pretty blurred so it might have been a bin liner caught in the branches but wasn't that – perched on the tower – *a big, long-necked, black bird?*

Twelve

Zed couldn't sleep and lay in bed with her shutters open, waiting for dawn, and her birthday. When she came down to the kitchen, Mum had left out cards from Granny Steph, Nanny Pam and Bethany. Zed ripped Beth's open and pulled out a dog with big goggle eyes and a silly hat. Beth wasn't allowed a pet and so she'd always been drawn to anything with dogs on. Her pencil case was a sausage dog, and when she was younger, although worryingly not that much younger, her duvet cover and pillows had been covered in 101 Dalmatians. Zed remembered a sleepover where instead of counting sheep they had tried to count the black and white dogs to see if there really were 101. There were only fifty-seven and a few heads or bottoms where some unlucky pups met the seam. Then two years ago she had switched it for a boy band. Luckily that was a very short-lived phase. It made Zed smile, remembering that awful bedding and Beth's giggles when she told her about literally dribbling over her pillowcase. The card made her smile too. She opened it slowly, teasing herself, holding off the joy of that big bubbly scrawl – but there was hardly any writing inside. She flipped it over and then back again.

Happy Birthday Zed, love you lots Bethany x

Just that.

Zed peered into the envelope for a letter, a note, anything else – but no, that really was it.

Where were the reams and reams of wishes for the next year and memories of the last? Where were the funny cartoons and annoying confetti that got everywhere? They always put that in – it was tradition. And she wasn't being funny, but where was the present?

Zed carefully slid the card back in the envelope, placed it on the table in front of her and watched as three fat tears splotched onto her address.

There *was* a present from Amy, though, and Zed hadn't expected that. She pulled off the homemade paper, lots of black squiggles on bits of kitchen towel, to find a big bag of sea salt fudge, a thick square pad of paper with geometric designs in lovely muted colours, and a book showing her how to make all sorts of things out of origami. Not just animals, but jewellery and tanks, vases and cameras. It had a whole section of things you could make out of dollar bills and really complicated projects involving multiple sheets of paper – the Taj Mahal, the Eiffel Tower and Yoda. Zed's fingers started twitching. She flicked through the book, trying to decide what to make first, chose a maroon and mustard yellow print and began folding a Pekin hen.

Half an hour later, when there was still no sign of anyone else, Zed opened the back door and looked across the road. She really didn't want to be alone and although it wasn't even eight o'clock, she knew her neighbour would have been up for at least a couple of hours. Buttons started barking before she'd reached the door.

'Come in, come in,' Cordelia shouted through the window. 'I've baked you a birthday cake! We can have it for breakfast.'

Now, cake for breakfast sounded just the sort of birthday treat that Zed liked. As soon as she pushed up the latch, a warm, fruity smell engulfed her.

'How did you know it was my birthday?'

'Your father told me.'

'Yum, stewed apples?' Zed asked while taking off her shoes.

'Apple cake and we shall have it with goat's curd,' said Cordelia, waving at a cloth tied up with string and dripping into the sink. That bit didn't sound quite so appealing.

'Do you know a guy called Denzil?' asked Zed as she sat down at the table.

'Humph. Who's asking?'

'Uh – me? I met him in the woods yesterday. He was sketching down by the river.'

'Tremelin woods? You mean our bit of river?'

'Yeah.'

'Last I heard he was squatting in a boat over the other side of Clewmor.'

'He was drawing cormorants.'

'Well, now, some things don't change, eh? That obsession has gone on longer than most! Though quite what he sees in those gruesome birds I'll never know.'

'He told me all about them. How clever they are. How you can find them all over the world and in stories and legends from all different cultures and–'

'Gargoyles! That's what they remind me of.'

'Well, that's kind of my way of thinking, but he said–'

'They're sinister!'

'Denzil said they brought fishermen luck.'

'Well, didn't bring Gawen much luck, did they?'

'I thought it was just me,' said Zed. 'But he, I mean Denzil, was pretty strange too, so he probably wasn't going to be the best person to convince me that I've got them all wrong. I mean there's something about them that's really, like, dark – and if he's right and they really do know stuff, or represent stuff, like bad stuff before it happens, then that really creeps me out!'

'Humph. Bit of a problem. Living here.'

'You're telling me!' said Zed.

Cordelia untied the cloth above the sink and squeezed out the last of the milky liquid into a bowl, which she put onto the floor for Buttons. He lapped it up with a great deal more enthusiasm than Zed thought she'd be able to muster.

'And what exactly is that?' she asked carefully. 'Curds, did you say? Like in *Little Miss Muffet?*'

'That's the one. It's like a very soft goat's cheese, creamy and delicious. And you can stop pulling that face until you've tried it.'

'So you know him then, Denzil?'

'Yes.'

'And?'

'Do you think now that you're fourteen you can ask twice as many questions?'

'I just wondered–'

'He's my great-grandson. And we had a falling out. Plain and simple.'

'So he's – Tamsin's brother?'

'Half-brother. Same mother, different fathers. And Denzil's was never around, not even at the start.'

'Oh,' said Zed. She knew it wasn't polite to ask anymore. Yet, she did so want to know.

'He's– I won't say trouble,' said Cordelia, 'that's not fair, because it's a condition or something, isn't it? But he's got problems, without a doubt. And it was hard on his mum. Right from a baby, if he didn't get his own way, he had monstrous meltdowns. I tell you, your sister has nothing on him! Problem was he was such a clever little so and so,' Cordelia sighed.

'He was quite friendly. Well, once he stopped being cross with me for disturbing the birds.'

'Oh, he's not a bad lad. Not at heart, but he's proud! Proud and stubborn. And I said something he didn't like, so that was that. He's not been up to see me since.'

When she'd made tea, Cordelia cut Zed a thick slice of the cake.

'That was Suki's favourite, when she lived here in the caravan. Denzil and Tamsin's mother that is.'

It was warm and gooey, more like a soft bread with apples and almonds on the top. Zed waited patiently, and a little nervously, as Cordelia spooned a big dollop of the curd on the side (fortunately not the top!), and then she plunged her spoon into the sticky mess. She had a couple of mouthfuls of the oozing, spicy apple first before risking the congealed white mass, but it was delicious. All of it. Super delicious. And she grinned at Cordelia.

'*Penn-Bloedh Lowen.*'

'Huh?' said Zed through a mouthful of cake.

'Happy Birthday in Cornish! *Yeck ez Dah.*'

Zed raised an eyebrow.

'That means *Good Health.*'

'Thank you,' said Zed, scooping up the last of the curd.

'And *Benna Sywes*, which means *May Blessings Follow.*' Cordelia nodded and took a bite of her cake. 'And I hope they do!'

'Ooh, I've brought you something,' said Zed as she pulled out the origami hen. 'I made it myself.'

'Well, well, isn't that fine?' said Cordelia. She picked it up gently by the beak and held it up to the light. 'Very fine, indeed.'

'My sister gave me a book and lots of paper.'

'Quite right.'

'It teaches you how to do the folding–'

'I'll put her up on the windowsill so she can see her relatives out in the garden. No one's given me a present in, let's see–' She stopped and turned slowly. 'Well now, maybe that explains it.'

'Explains what?' asked Zed.

'Why he got himself in such a grump. Maybe he meant it as a present! That would be just like him, not to admit to it.' She looked down at the floor.

'Who? What?' Zed was really lost.

'Denzil. He came up here one day with a painting. He used to come up to see me most days. He'd bring his cider, delicious it is, thick and syrupy and oh my goodness it can give you a headache if you aren't careful! And we'd have some of that with my bread and cheese of an evening. He'd do little things for me sometimes, if I was careful not to actually ask him, but just point them out, you know, little jobs around the house or in the garden. And he talked about his drawings and his precious birds. Then one day he brought up a painting. An oil, it was, of the river, down where I met you. I could see that, but the colours were all pinks and purples and golds. Ridiculous. The river isn't that colour. Maybe abroad – somewhere tropical, but not here. Not the Clew! He asked me what I thought of it and I told him.'

'So what happened?'

'He picked it up and left. And he hasn't been back since.'

Zed cleared the table and put the bowls in the sink, not because she was naturally tidy or even that helpful, but because she wanted to get near the cake that was on the draining board, and snaffle a few more crumbs.

'So, why did they bring Gawen bad luck?'

'Mmm?'

'The cormorants?'

'Well, I don't suppose they did. Not really. If anything, it was the other way round.'

'So they brought him good luck?'

'No, I meant he brought bad luck upon them. Or at least one of them, the one he'd adopted, but all this talk of luck, it was nothing to do with luck. It was to do with love and loss. He adored Kerra and she adored him. And when he lost her, he went mad. When you're left alone with strong emotions like that, they can become savage, unruly, more ferocious than the sea.' She was silent for a moment. 'But I suppose you could say the bird brought him luck to start with. He trained her, you see, like the Japanese do. To help him fish. That's right, it was a she, because he called her Eve. I remember now, how he'd tell the story. He'd been trying to tame her for months and finally she trusted him enough to let him tie a snare around her throat on Midsummer's Eve. So he named her, with a little ceremony, and then they went out fishing and the snare prevented her from swallowing her catch, the big ones anyway, so when she returned to the boat he'd remove the fish, hook it out of her throat, and keep it.

'So it was like a kind of tight collar?'

'Exactly. They used to fish a lot like that in Asia, apparently, but no one had ever done it in these parts. And he did very well out of it – so, yes, I suppose you could say the bird brought him luck.'

'So…?'

'Kerra drowned. She was out in the boat with him and the bird, as she often was, if she wasn't helping out my mother with milking the cows or looking after me. They were only a little beyond the harbour mouth when they were hit by a big wave. The way he told it, she just got washed over and never came up to the surface. He was frantic. He dived in, yelling her name and swam up and down for hours, begging and trying to make deals with his version of God, but to no avail. They never found the body and he never recovered. Didn't even try. He locked himself up in the boathouse and drank himself to death. It was Dicky Glynn's father that found him, but I was the one that found the bird. You see, I went down to the boathouse, after they'd taken Gawen away, looking for something of Kerra, but she wasn't there, of course, not even a little tiny part of her.

'What had happened to Eve?'

'The place stank of death. He hadn't killed her, just stopped caring. She'd starved to death in a filthy, stinking cage. Half of her wing had been eaten away. I didn't know whether she'd attacked herself in desperation or another animal had got through the bars of the cage, but it was a god awful mess. And her eye. That horrid green, gummy eye. Staring. Accusing. I screamed and screamed until someone found me. One of my brothers, I think. And they threw what was left of the bird out onto the slip and carried me home.'

'And the boathouse?'

'I told you. Shut up. Empty. No one wanted to go anywhere near it.'

'Until now.'

'That's right. Until now.'

Thirteen

When Zed got back home Mum and Dad were in the kitchen. Dad was leaning against the Aga, staring at his slippers. Mum was talking really fast, but in a low, jagged voice that rumbled indistinctly like distant trucks on a motorway. It changed as soon as she saw Zed though, into something tight and rather shrill.

'Morning, Birthday Girl!' She stood up and stumbled a little as she opened her arms for a hug. 'I was just trying to decide what kind of cake to bake you.' Her smile was way too big to be convincing.

'Isn't Dad going to do it in his oven? That's what he promised–'

Zed saw her parents exchange a glance.

'The oven seems to be playing up at the moment,' said Mum, 'but we've never baked a cake in a range so that's going to be fun! Now, chocolate, I think. Would that be okay?'

'What about all the people in Clewmor,' said Zed, 'won't they be expecting their bread?'

'Well, they'll have to wait,' said Dad gruffly. 'And the big regular order is on hold anyway.' He folded the paper and waved it at her. On the front page was a big picture of Clewmor Hall with the headline:

Hotel Shuts due to Virus Outbreak.

Zed took it and began reading:

> *Guests have been asked to leave and afternoon teas cancelled at Clewmor Hall following an outbreak of a suspected 'airborne virus'.*
>
> *A spokesperson for the Hotel said they have closed as a precautionary measure and to facilitate the identification and source of the outbreak. They are working in conjunction with the local Environmental Health Dept …*

'Okay. D'you want to open your present or what?' said Dad. 'Come on, it's up at the top. Although we're going to keep it in–'

'Shh, Shaun!' said Mum, 'you'll give it away.'

They went outside and traipsed up the steps. Someone had tied three balloons on the post at the top.

A hideous thought flashed through Zed's mind. They had the empty stable and were surrounded by fields and Dad was always on about fresh air and connecting with nature–

They got to the door and Mum said, 'Now shut your eyes!'

OMG! They haven't...

All that crap, and spending hours brushing manes and picking at manky hooves. Zed couldn't even be bothered to brush her own hair or keep her own fingernails in decent shape.

She gave herself a moment, took a breath and arranged her face to look – well, she definitely couldn't manage delighted, but horrified might seem a little ungrateful.

Fortunately, her acting skills weren't put to the test.

Balanced on top of two bales of hay was a shiny plastic orange kayak with a black fabric seat and a big paddle. And a bright yellow life jacket was draped over the lawnmower. She breathed out a huge sigh of relief.

That afternoon, when it was high tide, Zed, Dad and Mum managed between them to carry the kayak down to the river. Dad, rather than trying to direct operations as usual, was very quiet and just did as he was told, taking the bulk of the weight. It was awkward with the three of them because they couldn't get their feet into a rhythm and they wobbled and knocked their way along the path, under the viaduct and towards the boathouse. Once they got onto the slip, Dad turned back saying he'd go and make the cake. And as soon as he'd gone Mum sat down and began to cry.

'It's your birthday! Shh – I'm sorry–' she kept saying as she wiped away her tears on her sleeve.

'It's okay,' said Zed, kicking the ground, but it obviously wasn't.

'Everything is such bloody hard work. Relationships are such bloody hard work!' Mum carried on half laughing and half crying. 'You'll learn that, when you, you know–' She looked at Zed. 'I'm sorry,' she said, 'so much has gone on in the last few months, I mean with me, and me and dad, and Amy and Luke... You're always so – easy, and – well, I have no idea, do I? What's been going on in your life, Zed, and if there's anyone, you know, anyone special.'

Didn't see that one coming!

'You can always talk to me, like. You know that, don't you?'

Apparently not. Zed's throat went dry and tight, as if someone was crushing her neck like an empty can.

'Um–'

'I've not really been there for you–'

'Well–'

'But you seem to take everything in your stride, unlike the rest of us. Never giving us any trouble.'

Zed just stood there staring at the ground, trying to work and rework the words in her head. All she could manage, in a teeny tiny voice, was:

'What do you mean by *trouble*?'

'Oh, you know,' Mum tailed off. 'I worry about so many things–' then she tried to smile again. 'But tell me, I've always wondered, you and Kabir,' she leaned her body into Zed, giving her thigh a little nudge. 'Did anything happen? Before we left, I mean?'

'Mum–' Zed groaned.

'Go on! I know he always had a thing about you, it was obvious.'

Zed felt her face get hot. Really hot.

'Don't be embarrassed. He's a nice lad. I would have been thrilled to see you two get together, if we'd stayed, I mean. Was that him you were messaging yesterday?'

'Yes, but – he's just a friend!'

'Are you sure?'

'I want to get out onto the water, Mum.'

Mum grabbed Zed's leg and shook it. She was laughing, but her eyes were welling up again too. 'Come on, cheer up your poor old mam, with a little bit of uncomplicated romance.'

Zed pulled away, picked up the life jacket and stuffed the seat into the boat, attaching it with the four metal cleats. She shoved the kayak into the water and stepped in. There was a bit of a lurch while she sat down and worked out where to put her feet so that her knees were bent at the right angle, but it felt pretty stable. Amy had found her a couple of films to watch on her phone: a very irritating American blonde princess type assuring her it was all about getting the right twist in the torso and rotating the paddle, so that the blades were angled correctly when they entered the water.

'I mean, how hard can it be?' Zed had said to her sister. The answer was *not very*! Well, maybe out at sea, negotiating the waves around some big hunk of rock, but not floating with the tide, on the smooth, flat river.

Mum was standing up to her knees in the water watching rather anxiously. When she realised that Zed wasn't going to capsize, she pointed her toes and started tracing circles in the water.

'It's actually quite warm,' she called over to Zed, who was turning the boat around to try it out against the current. 'Do you think anyone comes down here? Apart from you and Cordelia?'

Zed thought of Denzil keeping his distance from Tremelin, and Dicky Glynne who had chosen to stay away all these years.

'You're alright, Mum,' she replied. 'It's just us. Are you coming in, then?'

'I haven't got a costume.'

'You could skinny dip!'

'I'm not sure, maybe another time.'

'Oh, go on!' said Zed. 'In your underwear then – you'll really enjoy it.'

Mum hesitated for a moment, then pulled her dress up over her head and threw it onto the bank. And with a series little yelps, she gingerly edged herself further out.

Zed went back and forward across the river several times. On the far side, when she got into the shallow water, she used the paddle to push herself against the riverbed like a punt. In this way she was able to hug the bank and manoeuvre herself along under a canopy of dead trees. Some of the chalky branches had torn away from the trunk and were dragging in the water, but if she leaned right back in her seat she could just get underneath. Glancing upwards, as she propelled herself through the tunnel of dead wood, she saw clumps of twigs tangled into the upper branches.

Nests! Oh hell...

Her mouth went dry. She forced herself to swallow and looked around, but there was nothing. Not even a duck, or a swan.

It was turning cold. And the sullen sky had taken on a purple tinge, like a faded bruise. Without the sunlight filtering through the trees, the brittle branches and derelict nests of this deserted colony felt pretty bleak. It reminded Zed of an elephants' graveyard.

And there, standing on a lump of granite by the bank, was a cormorant.

Zed couldn't move. An icy cramp shot down her leg and her hands went numb.

The cormorant was looking out over the water. It was so still it could have been a carved statue. Varnished. With a marble for an eye. That one lurid green eye, watching – watching–

Zed's chest began to burn. It felt stretched, swollen, and her heart pummelled against her lifejacket – and in her ears – and in her skull.

Long, slow breaths. Come on, now. Breathe...

She shuddered, remembering Eve, the bird Gawen trained and then left to starve.

The cormorant, as if sensing her discomfort, and revelling in it, turned its head in a succession of little jolts until it was facing her, its direct stare a kind of challenge.

Cordelia was right, there was something monstrous about it. Something reptilian.

Zed stared back. Not out of defiance, but because a kind of fog had paralysed her brain.

The cormorant blinked, dipped its beak in a slow nod and with a deep, piggy grunt, it was off, beating the air above her.

Zed threw her hands up over her head, squeezed her eyes shut and sank into the boat. When she looked out from under her elbow, she could see it gliding towards the boathouse. It landed on the slip for a moment, squawked and took off again, disappearing up the creek.

Mum had been swimming in circles with a sort of lopsided breaststroke.

'Your dad was right. I should do this every day,' she said when Zed got herself together and paddled back across the river. 'Where's the best place to get out, do you think?'

'Well, the boathouse is the only place you won't get covered in mud.'

Mum swam up the creek and Zed paddled along behind. When they reached the slipway, Mum clambered up, her bottom sticking in the air as she half crawled, trying to get a grip on the mossy stones. She stood carefully and took a couple of tentative steps, before reaching for a branch–

And she fell.

Not a stumble or a slide, it was cleaner than that: her feet just went from underneath her. There was a moment when she shrieked and tried to grab the branch again, but her hand just groped the air and she had nothing to break her fall. She went down hard, almost bouncing off the granite.

Zed yelled, 'Mum. Mum, are you okay? Mum?'

The silence stretched – and then a moan.

Zed frantically paddled towards the boathouse and then scrambled out of the kayak, dragging it far enough in to prevent it floating away. She reached for Mum's leg, shaking it gently.

'Mum?'

'It's alright love, just give me a moment.' She slowly raised herself onto one hip. She'd cut her head, just above the brow, and blood had trickled into her ear and wet hair and then, diluted, it gushed down her face and dripped off her chin. She'd scraped the skin off her cheekbone too and all up the outside of her left arm, where more blood mingled with green algae and mud. As she carefully twisted herself onto her bottom, she yelped.

'Ouch. Bloody, bloody – ouch!'

She tried to flex her foot and yelped again. Zed knelt down beside her and went to put her hand under her armpit to help lift her up. Mum flinched though and Zed pulled back.

'What can I do?' Zed asked, feeling very helpless.

Mum exhaled slowly though pursed lips.

'Perhaps – could you find my dress?'

Mum edged her way up the slip on her bottom and managed to pull herself upright, with the help of some thick tendrils of ivy. She stood on one leg in her saggy bra and knickers. She looked like she'd been in a fight.

They lifted the dress carefully over her head and tugged it down where it clung to her sodden underwear. She was covered in goose bumps.

'Can you lean on me?' asked Zed.

'I'm going to have to,' said Mum.

If Zed thought the journey to the boathouse was slow and difficult, the journey home was going to take all night. Mum draped her arm around Zed's shoulders and hobbled as best she could, but she needed to stop and rest every few steps and they made very little progress. They were both getting cold.

'Why don't you sit down and wait, and I'll get Dad?' said Zed.

She ran home as fast as she could and found Dad sitting in the bakery. When she told him what had happened, he grabbed a blanket and together they ran back and found Mum lying in a foetal position on the ground. Her teeth were chattering, but she attempted a reassuring smile. Dad wrapped her in the blanket, carefully lifted her up and carried her back up the path. Cordelia, alerted by the commotion, was waiting by the viaduct with a hip flask of brandy.

'Have a swig of that, Lucy,' she said, holding it out.

Mum did as she was told. Gulped, swallowed, grinned weirdly and was sick all over Dad's fleece.

After a bath, some hot sugary tea that stayed down, and some mega painkillers Dad had for his back, they tucked her up in bed with her ankle raised up on a pile of cushions and wrapped in a tea towel full of crushed ice. Dad wanted to call out the doctor, but Mum convinced him that it wasn't necessary. The bruising was already coming out under the anklebone, like a smear of blackberry juice, and the swollen flesh above was the colour of wax. It was springy to touch.

Their first aid box was pretty sparse, but Cordelia brought over a bottle of iodine, which had long since lost its label and was crusty around the rim, and after much swearing, from nurse and patient, Zed managed to clean up Mum's arm and face. Mum then leaned back, shut her eyes and quickly fell asleep.

Dad just hovered in the doorway.

And he never did make the cake.

Fourteen

It was dusk when Zed got back down to the river. Although the tide was low, it would come back in overnight and there was nothing to secure the kayak. It would probably float away if she didn't get it inside the boathouse, or it could be stolen. Did she have to worry about things like that here? Well, it was still on the bank, so not today it seemed. There were plenty of other things to worry about.

The boat was a long way above the water level now, as were the muddy skid marks cutting through the green gunge where Mum had fallen. To get the kayak inside the boathouse, she needed to open the double doors at the top of the slip, and it took Zed a moment to work out which of the three keys released the rusty padlock. Even when she had inserted the right one, she struggled to rotate it. Her hands were shaking, and she kept glancing into the bushes. She twisted and pulled the key out again and then spat on it before pushing it back into the cylinder. That seemed to work and with a tug she got the padlock open. Zed hauled back the door on the right, dragging it over the stones, and peered inside. It was hard to see anything in the murky light, but she located an old bolt at floor level and once she had released that, she was able to pull back both doors as far as they would go.

She put her hands on her hips, but in a moment they were back at her sides; tensed, flexed and ready.

Cordelia had said that Kerra wanted to make this her home, made it out to be some kind of love nest. *Yeah, right!*

Zed turned and began to edge her way down the slip until she was level with the bow of the kayak. She reached for the handle and pulled it towards her. It came easily, sliding over the wet grass. Crouching down, she managed to get far enough underneath to ease it over the trench between the bank and the slipway, and then by wriggling to one side she was able to lower it, with only a small bump, onto the stones. She was pulling it up the slip, when the first belch in the bushes jolted her forwards. It was echoed immediately by another, further away, and then another close by, almost overhead. She knew that sound. She gave the boat a last violent tug onto the flat and then, as fast as she could, she shoved it through the boathouse doors, along the ground until it came to rest beside the rowing boat. She edged her way back to the entrance, and cowering under the slate overhang, her back pressed up against the doorframe, she peered up into the trees. How many were out there? Three? Four? They were very close.

She pulled the first door shut and twisted the bolt from side to side as fast as she could, forcing it down into the ground. Once secure, she reached for the second door and was swinging it back towards her when–

'Jeez!' Zed screamed.

She yanked the door, not shut, but enough – and heard a violent thud as the bird hit the wood. It fell to the ground, staggered and slipped. Pumping its wings, straining its neck, it tried to lift itself off the ground again, then stumbled into the bushes, screeching. And then another – diving towards her. A thick black dart coming straight at her. Its beak an open compass, shiny and sharp on either side of a gaping black hole. She ducked, hands over her face, and it swerved off to the left at the last moment. Through her fingers she could see its open beak silhouetted against the sky; a pair of hooked tweezers – Zed yanked the door again, as hard as she could, but it was snagging on some loose shingle. She kicked the grit out of the way and pulled the door shut just in time as a third shrieking bird threw itself at her, with such ferocity that it dented the rotting door; pushing the pulpy wood into a bulge that she could feel under her hand as she pressed herself against the inside.

What the hell...?

She flung herself to the far end of the building, nearly tripping over Dad's outboard motor and crouched down in the corner by the stove. She could hear them on the roof, their shrill squawks cutting through the dull thuds of their feet and wings. It was getting louder and louder, the thumping blending like the rain had in the storm. That call, ripped from deep inside their guts.

Then a crash; shattered glass flung into the room. Zed twisted her neck and tried to squeeze sideways between the boat and the wall, but she couldn't breathe.

Please not this again...

There were sparks fizzing inside her eyelids. Red, hot spits on her hands and face–

Breathe... just breathe...

It felt like scalding sparklers scoring her skin, dragging it into blisters. Her throat was tight. Her chest was tight. She couldn't get enough air.

Self in a tiny, sizzling, crunched up ball, rolling away...

And then a hit of oxygen, and the soft beating of wings, like someone shaking out a rug, followed by silence. The cormorants were gone.

Zed didn't move. For how long, she couldn't have said. It felt like hours before the blood stopped pulsing in her ears and the pounding in her chest softened. She waited until the stiffness in her legs became more unbearable than the thought that the cormorants might come back, before crawling out from behind the boat.

There was still enough light for her to see the outlines of the trees reflected in the shards of glass lying in the hull. Something else caught her eye. Lying on the floor, just underneath the window, was a small leather band. It was curled around on itself and fastened with a smooth metal stud, pushed up though a roughly punctured hole. It wasn't very big.

A child's bracelet?

It hadn't been there before.

She picked it up and stuffed it into the pocket of her dungarees before pulling out her phone. Maybe Amy would come and – but of course, there was no signal, not one measly bar.

Okay, a weapon then.

She picked up a deck chair and held it up in front of her. She looked at the rotten canvas and dismissed that idea. What about an oar? Something to hit with – if, if – but an oar would slow her down. If she went through the trees, kept low and wove in and out of the undergrowth, alongside the path, but not actually on it, then at least they couldn't fly at her.

Now. Before the last light fades.

She opened the side door, took a big gulp of air, and started to run.

Fifteen

Zed knocked on Amy's door.

'Ames?'

'Yeah. What d'ya want?'

'Um, well, I wanted to say thanks again, for my presents. They're really–'

Without looking up, Amy replied. 'Yeah, whatever.'

'And also–' Zed was still standing in the doorway. 'Can I–' The sob came from nowhere.

'Are you on your period? Again?'

'No! It's not that.'

'Oh crap! Well you'd better come in.'

'That sounds pretty sinister,' she said when Zed had finished, but in a way that made it sound like it could actually be quite exciting. Zed was so grateful to be in a thick walled, warm, dry house however, and with someone who believed her, that she didn't challenge her. Even though she couldn't see anything exciting about it at all.

'No wonder you're spooked!' said Amy, who'd already invited Zed to sit on the bed next to her, and now gave her a quick hug. Her hair was so stiff with products and her body so bony, that it felt like being cuddled by a broomstick.

'And it sounds like you had some kind of panic attack. Though I'm not surprised, in the circumstances.'

'It isn't the first time.'

'It's like some badass horror story!'

'Don't tell me, Luke would love it,' said Zed, wiping her nose on her sleeve.

Amy pulled away.

'Yeah, well–'

Zed looked at her.

'Yeah well, what?'

'Luke can be a jerk.'

It was so hard not to agree that Zed had to stuff one of Amy's cushions into her mouth. It was furry and in a moment her tongue was covered in fluff.

'I'm actually beginning to wish he'd get off my case,' Amy continued. 'He seems to think I have a choice, that I don't have to be here! So, either he's shouting at me and telling me that if I cared about him I'd pack my bags and get on a coach, or he goes all moody and silent. I mean, he'll say he wants to chat, but then just sits there like a douchebag: staring at me and fiddling with his roll-ups. Like that's going to make us feel better!'

'At least he *wants* to talk to you. Beth is always so busy–'

'I prefer the shouting,' said Amy, twisting her mouth, so it was hard for Zed to tell if she was attempting a sardonic smile or trying to hold back tears herself. 'It's not so bad on a screen! At least he's trying to communicate – with words. At least then it seems like he cares enough to want to try and make me go back. Turn down the volume and that actually feels really nice, that he cares that much, that I can make such a difference to how someone feels.'

Zed nodded. She got that. To be number one, for someone, anyone actually, must feel pretty good.

It's what Kerra and Gawen had, right? Obviously it didn't work out so great for them, but to have that must be pretty special.

'The silent moody treatment sucks though. The zoning out. It's like he can't be bothered anymore. And we're getting it from Dad too!' said Amy. 'I mean, look at him. What's that all about?'

'He's just a bit down.'

'Exactly my point. All those months of telling me that Luke moped around like a loser and who's doing it now?'

'At least he's not smoking roll-ups!' said Zed with a grin. 'Although obviously homemade would be better than out of a packet!'

'But what I don't get, is why the sudden change of heart? One minute he's all over the crazy baker routine, fresh starts, new life, yabba, yabba, yabba – and now it's like he's been kicked in the nuts.'

'He'll be better in a few days.'

'You think? At least when he was always away we didn't have to witness the whole misery act! When it's Mum who's down – it's kind of dignified. And I can cope with Mum because she's not always telling us what to do, but Dad is such a knob. Anyway, he's not my problem, but when it's Luke doing the whole distant cool thing, well, that feels like he *is* my problem.'

'Aren't you worried about Mum?'

'Yeah, of course, but she's got to sort it.'

'What if she can't?'

They sat in silence for a bit, until Zed said, 'So, what would Luke say about the cormorants?'

Amy rolled her eyes. 'Oh, you know, they're some kind of murdering shape shifters out to get you.'

'Great,' said Zed. 'That makes me feel a whole lot better!'

Sixteen

Zed had to pick up her bike from Clewmor. Tamsin had rung twice and left messages, but she'd been putting it off because it was a long walk, and she was hoping to get a lift in. She wanted to arrive in town looking fresh and radiant, well, as radiant as she could with blackheads and braces, but there was no point asking Dad, the mood he was in, and Mum was definitely going to be resting for a while. She was lying in her bedroom with the shutters pulled to and had been ever since they'd brought her back from the boathouse. The cut above her eyebrow had closed up, but was still very tender, her arm was badly bruised under the scabs and her elbow was red and swollen where she'd knocked it.

'How are you feeling?' asked Zed when she took her a cup of tea and an origami frog. Mum ignored the question, the tea and the gift, and just lay there staring at the strip of light between the shutters.

Zed peeled back the corner of the duvet. 'Your ankle looks less puffy. That's something.'

'Something–' Mum echoed.

'What?'

'Something? Or nothing?' she said very quietly.

'Mum?'

'Is there something out there? D'you think?'

'Um. Are we talking big picture stuff here, or just what's knocking around Tremelin?'

'Both, I guess.' She turned and looked at Zed. Her pupils were massive. 'I'm sorry, my head's chocka and it hurts!' she whispered.

'I'm not surprised,' said Zed.

'It hurts all the time!'

'Mum, I need some cash. I've got to pick up my bike.'

It seemed to take her a moment to process Zed's words.

'Pass my bag.'

Zed walked over to the chest of drawers where Mum's favourite leather bag was bulging open, stuffed full of papers, receipts, lipsticks, and a sheet of pills.

'Have you had some of these?' Zed asked.

'Could you give it to me?'

Zed hesitated. 'Have you had any today?'

'No.'

Zed popped two pills into the palm of her hand, walked back to the bed and handed Mum a glass of water.

'There are some notes in my purse,' said Mum. 'I know what you're like with money, so put them somewhere safe.'

'Of course,' said Zed, raiding the purse and stuffing the contents into her pocket.

Mum leaned back against her pillow, winced and shut her eyes.

'And I'm expecting some change.'

Zed took her time, going via a café first, to spend some of Mum's money.
Well, it's important to have a good breakfast, right?

Afterwards she used their loo and checked herself in the mirror, put her hair up, let it down again, changed the position of her parting, and ran her hands through it so it looked less, well, *styled,* then set off for the bike shop.

Bill smiled and nodded as soon as she appeared in the doorway.

'Alright?' he said. 'Tams 'ad your wheel done for you a few hours after you left. We was wonderin' where you'd got to. An' we might need that for one of the holiday lets,' he said, pointing at the hire bike.

'Sorry,' said Zed.

'I'd seen your dad handing out his bread all over town, but I didn't put two and two together. Didn't know that you were the ones moved in opposite Suki's Gran.'

'Yep, that's us,' said Zed.

'Used to go up that way a lot when Suki and me got together,' he said, tapping a spanner against the heel of his thumb. 'She lived in Tremelin with her son.'

'Denzil?'

'That's 'im. And she moved back out to Cordelia's afterwards, you know – when it didn't work out.'

'Yes, I um, heard that,' said Zed. She felt a bit light-headed and her conversational skills were not exactly razor sharp.

'Was the worst thing she could 'ave done, looking back on it. It's a lovely place, don't get me wrong, but not if you're strugglin'.'

The shop seemed awfully quiet.

'Probably not my biggest fan, Cordelia. Seemed to think it was my fault that things went wrong. Even though I'm the one bringin' up Tams and her granddaughter's the one that's done a runner, but there's no point arguin' with 'er!'

Where is Tamsin? Out probably, with her friends.

'Was the day after the storm, wasn't it, that you 'ad your accident? That's right! You an' Tristo. Same day. An' you know what?' he said, frowning. 'That was the start of it, a run of bashed-up bikes! Good for us, mind. I dunno, folks gone crazy this summer.'

'Right. Well–'

'An' this morning we hear that Mr Cardew be the one who's been throwin' pots of paint all over town! It's unbelievable! All week, we've been wakin' up to it. Paint all over the bus stop an' the front door of the post office, big splats of the stuff all down Fore Street an' slopped over the tables outside The Ship, an' everyone grumblin'! Not surprisin', mind, not easy to get paint off.'

'No, I'm sure–'

'But no one could have guessed it be him! Some young troublemaker maybe – but he's an old man, dear of 'im, a widower quietly getting on with life! Doin' 'iss bit of Bed & Breakfast, you know, it's the one by the church.'

'He was caught, fair an' square, Dad.' And Tamsin walked in from the workshop at the back. She was holding an enormous mug that said *The Boss*.

'Yes, I know he was,' Bill carried on. 'Doreen filmed it on 'er new phone. Dead chuffed she was to 'ave caught the culprit, but who would 'ave thought Mr Cardew would be the vandal! When the police came, he said he didn't know what he was doing. Said he'd been sleepwalkin'.'

'So, about time!' said Tamsin, looking at Zed. 'Is this what is meant by being fashionably late?'

'To be late there has to be an agreed time in the first place. And I don't believe we ever did agree one. So not late exactly – either fashionably or otherwise!' *Nice one Zed! Now your soon-to-be classmate is going to add unbearably pompous to her list of grievances.* 'But I am sorry if you needed your bike back,' she added hastily.

Tamsin grinned. 'Okay, you got a point, but, hey, chill ya boots–' *Who actually says chill your boots?* 'So, does it feel like home, yet? Up there in Tremble-in?' She was not exactly smirking, but it was near enough.

'We're, um – getting there.'

'Fighting talk, I like that,' she said, sipping her tea. 'So where *are* you from then? Your mum sounds different to you.'

'She's from Liverpool and if you think that's different, you should hear my nan! We grew up in London, though.'

'Uh, huh. As I thought, city girls through and through.' *Here we go again.* 'But Cordelia's given you the thumbs up. So I guess I'll give you the benefit of the doubt too.'

'You're *very* kind,' said Zed. It sounded even more sarcastic than she had intended, and she quickly glanced at Tamsin, to check they weren't back to square one.

Wow, what a smile!

'The bike looks great,' Zed blurted out. She focused on the invoice taped to the handlebars and clumsily counted out the right money. 'Thank you and, um–' She had to turn away, unable to meet Tamsin's gaze again, 'I *am* sorry I didn't come back sooner.'

'No worries. Dad's was only flapping because the workshop is so crammed.'

Zed nodded, and wheeled the bike to the door, trying hard not to knock into anything, or trip over the tools lying on the floor.

'You know, if you think you really are gonna stay, you should start taking an interest in the local environment.'

Zed turned around.

'What? How do you mean?'

'Well, if you're around later, there's a group of us going down to clean up the beach,' Tamsin said while licking her fingertip and running it along her eyebrow.

'Right–'

'It's a *Surfers against Sewage* type thing. Not that there's that much surf, round here, but y'know – the beach is a tip.'

'What, like litter and stuff?'

'Yes. Some of it's just people not taking their rubbish home and we've been clearing that up for a while, but this is different. In the last week or so, all sorts of minging stuff keeps washing up onto the shore. And no one knows where it's coming from.'

'Sounds horrible.'

'You should read our blog about it, *Birds in the Bladderwrack.* Give me your number an' I'll ping you a link.'

'It's no wonder, 'alf the town be puttin' their houses on the market,' said Bill, shaking his head. 'Second homers too! Not that us locals will be able to afford 'em, mind.'

'I'll see,' said Zed, concentrating on typing. 'Do you mean the beach out by the castle?'

'Yeah, that's the one. We meet up three times a week, Mondays, Wednesdays and Fridays. Sometimes we go to other beaches, further along the coast, but at the moment we're sticking with trying to clear that one.'

'I'll do my best,' said Zed.

That smile again.

'Sweet. See ya then.'

Zed wheeled the bike outside and was just coming back to close the door when she saw that Tamsin was still leaning against the doorframe of the workshop, watching her. There was something in her look that made Zed feel hot and full of caffeine and sugar.

'Something else?'

'I've met your brother,' said Zed.

Tamsin pushed herself upright and came towards the door.

'Denzil? Where? Where did you see him?'

'In the woods.'

'What, up by you?'

'Yes.'

'Does Cordelia know? Why didn't she tell me? She knew I'd been looking for him.'

'I only met him a couple of days ago. She seemed as surprised as you when I told her.'

'Is he sleeping rough?'

'What? In the woods? I don't know. It didn't, I didn't–'

'How was he?'

'Well, he's, um, a bit–'

'Strange. Yeah, sure, but did he seem okay?'

Tamsin didn't seem to know what to do with her hands. She kept putting them in her pockets and taking them out again.

'Well, he's very, um, enthusiastic. He told me some stories–'

'Yeah, he likes stories. He's good at telling stories. In fact, he's brilliant at telling stories.'

'And sort of acting them out?' said Zed uncertainly.

Tamsin grinned. 'That's part of it, apparently, role play an' that, escaping into his own little world, to avoid stuff, you know?'

Zed didn't really know, but she just nodded and tried her best to smile reassuringly.

'If you see him again, will you tell me? He can be a little git, but I still like to look out for him.'

'Yeah, sure.'

'He doesn't have anyone else, not really. Well, there's mum, but she's pretty flaky – and we're not quite sure where she is at the moment, to be honest. Her kind of surfing is couch surfing an' that's on a good day.'

'Of course,' said Zed.

Tamsin stepped forward, hesitated for a moment, then put her arms around her. Just briefly. Just enough for Zed to get a whiff of coconut and bike oil.

'Thanks,' she said, then turned and went back into the shop.

Zed leaned back on a bollard to steady herself.

Was that a... hug?

She pushed her bike up Fore Street. It wasn't much of a hill, but it was enough. She stopped for a moment and glanced at the window display in the surf shop. She needed some sunglasses – maybe something with a bit of swag – and if she was going to start going to the beach with Tamsin and her friends, she'd need a new bikini, an all-over suntan... and some serious therapy.

Not much to get sorted then.

Seventeen

As soon as Zed lifted her bike over the stile, she began to feel her stomach clench. It was the middle of the day and the shadows were short and squat, but any shadows were a bad thing, and it really wasn't going to take much to spook her.

She followed the path down towards the river, freewheeling, but slowly; her fingers gently squeezing the brakes. They didn't squeak anymore, that was a bonus. Tamsin had done more than just fix her wheel. Imagine if she buckled it again though, that would be so embarrassing. Tamsin would think she was such a jerk, or worse, that Zed had done it deliberately as an excuse to go and see her. She wasn't that desperate to make friends.

So Zed was looking out for rocks and fallen branches on the footpath, but she kept glancing into the undergrowth too; peering through the thick tangles of brambles and shin-spearing holly. The ivy, not content with strangling the trees, had crept out onto the path; its tendrils lying in wait, underneath the thin covering of leaves.

Her palms felt clammy against the rubber of her handlebars. She flexed her fingers and forced herself to look skywards.

Were the cormorants up there? Watching her?

Bill said lots of weird things started happening the day after the storm. Accidents, people going crazy, all the rubbish washing up on the beach – Denzil had seen the cormorants that night too, acting strangely, attacking each other, he said, drawing blood.

What was that?

Zed froze, her feet abandoning the pedals for the woodland floor. She was poised to throw her bike aside. If she had to make a break for it, she'd be better on foot. Faster. She'd need her hands free too.

She heard it again. Something moving in the bushes, a crunching noise, heavy breathing–

She screamed.

'Wooooa. Who's that?'

It was Denzil. He trudged out from behind a tree stump, carrying his sketchpad and a canvas bag. He stopped right in front of her, blocking the path.

'You're lookin' pretty w-w-wisht today!' he said, frowning.

'Wisht?' replied Zed, weakly.

'Pale! Like you've 'ad a fright.'

'Fright?'

'Why are you c-c-copyin' everythin' I say?' He pulled on his beard, twice, and tilted his head.

Zed took a deep breath. 'No, I've not had a fright, apart from you of course, at least not today.'

'What's that face for then?' said Denzil. 'S...s...seen a ghost?' He leaped to the side of the path and crouched down behind a tree stump and called in a little faraway voice, 'Welcome to Tremelin, you must be exhausted and hungry after your journey. Please join us for a feast.' And he grabbed a fist full of nettles and thrust it towards her.

'Doesn't that sting?' said Zed.

'A non-believer, huh?' said Denzil in his normal voice. 'You'll r...regret that!'

'Look, I am actually a bit tired!'

'I reckon there be plenty of ghosts round these p-p-parts. An' they can show themselves in all sorts of different ways.'

'Well, I didn't see a ghost,' said Zed, choosing her words carefully, 'but I did experience something very odd the other day and it's left me feeling a little anxious so if you don't mind–'

'What?' said Denzil, rolling the nettles and then popping them in his mouth. 'What did you see?'

Zed sighed, 'The cormorants, like you said, in the thunderstorm – the cormorants – well, I was in the boathouse, you know, down near us, and they – they attacked me. Like, properly attacked me. It was terrifying, they–'

'Why?'

'I've no idea. I've done nothing to hurt them!'

'Well,' he said with a grunt, 'someone must 'ave done!'

'I thought, maybe you–'

'An' it sounds like it's your job to make peace!'

Denzil said he would walk with her. Not as far as Tremelin, but a bit of the way, what with her being so jittery.

'There are lots of b-blackthorn b-bushes over that side of the woods an' I wouldn't mind seein' if any s...s...sloes 'ave appeared yet.'

Zed wasn't convinced that being alone with Denzil for any length of time was the answer to calming her nerves, but she got off her bike anyway and walked alongside him.

'What were you drawing today?' she asked politely.

He shook his head. 'Mainly snoozin'. 'Ad a mug or two of cider last night, didn't I? Was bleddy good stuff.'

'So, your dad's a b-b-baker then?' he said after a bit.

Ha – almost like polite conversation.

'He was hoping to be,' replied Zed, 'but he seems to have lost interest.'

'Go on! I 'eard he was makin' all sorts and gonna sell 'em round town?'

'That was the plan,' said Zed, 'but I don't know if he still thinks it's such a good idea. I'm not even sure he thinks us being here is such a good idea anymore. He makes all these plans, but then–'

'Then what?'

'Sometimes he – sort of, runs out of steam.'

'Was it his idea to get you d-down 'ere?'

'Yes.'

'Well, you're 'ere. So he s...saw that one through.'

'Yes, but–'

'An' was it such a daft idea?'

Zed thought about that for a moment. 'Well, things aren't going so well right now, but I guess I won't be able to answer that properly until school starts. And it depends if Mum is still on board. She didn't want it to be a daft idea, I know that. She was definitely up for it to start with. And Amy, well–'

'Ah yes, your s...s...sister! I 'eard she's some heller.'

'Heller?'

'A troublesome one,' said Denzil with a grin. 'Like me.'

'She just didn't want to be dragged away from her boyfriend to live in the middle of nowhere. She's good at art though. Like you.'

Denzil raised one eyebrow, but said nothing, for a bit, and then, 'Sometimes you got to have faith in your p-p-parents, your mum an' dad, like the cormorants do. Hatchlings of game birds always be starvin' or fallin' out of the trees, but not cormorant chicks. They be kept safe in their nests for as long as possible. Their p-p-parents go out an' gather food, eat it an' come back to the nest.'

Denzil pushed his bag back over his shoulder and lifted both his hands up, the fingers and thumbs pressed together. He started making little squeaking noises and twisting his wrists. He turned to Zed and said, 'Then they open their jaws, really wide, an' the little ones put their heads right inside to get their dinner. That's proper trust, that is! The b-b-babes are all wrigglin' and it looks like they're bein' swallowed, but they're not, they're bein' given what they need.'

He opened his mouth really wide, like a silent scream, and pushed both his hands in until he started to gag. He pulled them out, shiny with saliva and jabbed them towards Zed. 'An' trustin' their parents, even though they might 'ave flown off for a bit an' come back squawking or pecking at 'em, it's the only way it's goin' to work. It's the only way they'll stay s...s...safe an' grow up big an' strong.'

'Well, it doesn't sound like *your* mum is doing what's best for you!' said Zed, stumbling backwards and hating herself almost straight away.

'What you 'eard about my m...m...mum?' He looked really angry now and the chicks turned into fists.

'Well, she's not around, is she?'

'My mum knows what's right for me!' he shouted. 'It wasn't right for her, moving back up to Tremelin, but she knew it was right for me, so she came anyway. Like them birds sacrificin' their dinner.'

'But where is she now?' said Zed, knowing as the words came out that she was just digging herself in deeper.

He leaped forward and lifted his arms up as if he was going to grab her, but he pushed his chest forward and shook them out in a series of little jolts.

'You have to face your fears in the woods,' he hissed. 'That's how you sort yourself out. She knew the peace and quiet, drawing, no one hasslin' me, that was gonna make me feel better – and she was right. She looked after me when it mattered. And now, maybe it's her time to do what she wants for a bit.'

'Okay, okay– I'm sorry.'

'An' maybe it was too much for her, all that quiet, all that thinking time. An' bein' alone so much, or just with me – but she didn't leave until she could, you know, not 'til I could look after meself. And Tams 'as got 'er dad.'

They were within sight of the viaduct now and Denzil suddenly dropped his arms and shuffled over to the side of the path.

'Don't think I'll be goin' much further, don't know who might be out walkin'.'

Zed wasn't going to argue.

'There's the sloes,' he said, pointing over to a spiky bush, covered in little green berries. 'They'll be ripenin' a bit early this year what with all the rain. I reckon I'll be back when they're ready. Collect a bag or two to make my gin. Now go home.'

'Thank you. For, you know, walking with me,' said Zed awkwardly.

''Ere,' he said, getting down on his knees and pulling his sketchbook out of his bag. He ripped out a page, then another and another.

'Oh don't–' said Zed, but he ignored her. When he'd finished, he rolled them up into a tube and reached across, jabbing them into her chest.

'Read it!' he said. Then he nodded, turned around and started plodding back up the path, but he stopped after a few paces and looking straight ahead into the trees, he said, 'Does she still 'ave the little one? Buttons?'

It took Zed a moment to realise who he meant.

'Yes, and two goats, four cats and a lot of chickens.'

'Good,' he replied. 'It's good for her to 'ave c-c-company.' And off he went.

When she got home, Zed got out her phone. Tamsin hadn't messaged her yet, but she'd mentioned a blog, hadn't she? Something about seagulls and seaweed? No, *birds*, that was it.

> ### BirdsintheBladderwrack
> *Four girls making a difference. One ripple at a time.*

Zed went straight to the gallery. She scrolled back to the start where there were idyllic photos of golden sands, sunsets and girls in wetsuits, splashing around in the waves. Tamsin was easy to spot as the others all had dark hair. There were films of beach parties, beach cricket and kite surfers interspersed with pictures of rubbish collected, a pile of cigarette butts, and an old burnt out car. There was a page about plastic free picnics, with lots of ideas for things you could bring with no packaging (Dad would like that!) and there was a *Hey there, this is us!* page where Tamsin, Bella, Mimi and Jim (who was definitely female – with a wetsuit on you couldn't ignore her curves) introduced themselves. Tamsin's bit was really short. It was a picture of her on a windy day, in a thick red jumper and woolly scarf, with her hair blowing across her face, in fact you couldn't really see her face at all, but it was definitely her. Then there was a list down the side:

> ### Give me five–
> *bikes*
> *beaches*
> *bobble hats*
> *banana peanut butter smoothies*
> *and babes!*

The blog itself was mainly written by Bella. It was funny, but pretty punchy too; she was definitely on a mission.

> *There are 51 trillion microplastic particles polluting our world's seas! For the Dude who said to me last night, 'yeah whatevs, let's just let the universe take care of itself and make tunes in the dunes under that beautiful night sky', that's 500 times more*

than the stars we have in our galaxy. Put that in your bong and smoke it!

But she'd written three posts in the last week that weren't funny at all. They were all were accompanied with photos and Zed was shocked by the banks of rubbish and sludge, the volume of plastic, bits of netting, rope and old clothes that had been found on Clewmor Beach. The last post, written the previous day, said:

> *What has happened to our beautiful coastline? Am I the only one thinking that our lack of respect for the natural world is coming back to bite us? We need to live in harmony with our planet because nature is cleverer, more complex and way more resourceful than we give it credit for. It's as if Mother Nature, Gaia or however you want to refer to the life force of our planet (she's a woman, obvs!) has finally found a way to chuck back at us all the crap we've been flinging at her for way too long. It's as if she's said, 'Enough, guys. This is war!'*

Zed went back to Tamsin's photo, then messaged her.

> *Hey Tamsin, on my way home and just seen Denzil in woods again. Said I'd let you know.*

She typed two kisses, deleted them, put one back again – and pressed *send*.

THE CORMORANTS
OF UDROST

ONCE UPON A TIME there was a poor fisherman who had far too many children, but he loved them all and he worked hard to keep them fed and clothed.

He never moaned and despite his daily struggle to make ends meet, he was always generous, kind and very grateful for what he had.

His neighbor was a rich man who never stopped moaning! He even grumbled about the fisherman and his family because their hut ruined his view of the water.

At night when the fisherman, his wife and children were laughing and singing, their neighbor sat in his big house plotting ways to get rid of them.

83

One day in early autumn the neighbor called 'It's a lovely day, if I were you, I'd go right out to sea.' The fisherman looked up at the sky. He was pretty sure a storm was coming, but his neighbour assured him the forecast was fine, so he set off.

It wasn't long before a thick fog descended and he lost his bearings.

'Which way is home?' he wondered desperately. The sky rumbled and a vicious gale lashed his tiny boat, washing water over the deck. The fisherman gripped the tiller, hoping to keep the boat straight, but he didn't stand a chance against the howling wind and the torrential rain.

He wept, thinking of the family he'd be leaving destitute.

'It seems like my neighbour's prayers have been answered, but I, too, can pray,' he said.

He prayed that he would reach land safely, and if not, this family would find a way to support themselves without him.

The fisherman heard a loud squawk. He peered through the sheets of rain, expecting to see some kind of monster, and in the distance he could see something black. His boat was heading right toward it, so he squeezed his eyes shut, but as he got closer he couldn't help peeking. Sitting on a piece of driftwood, were three cormorants.

Suddenly he felt the boat lurch to one side and grind to a halt. It was land

'It's a miracle! I'm saved!' he cried, jumping out. And as abruptly as it had started the storm ended. The late afternoon sky turned bright pink and the Fisherman discovered he was in the most peaceful place in the world, luscious green woodlands with banks of wild garlic and blackthorn trees covered in sloes.

In the distance were fields filled with prancing white goats. As he took it all in, the sun sank, and the whole landscape began to glow as if it had been dipped in gold. The Fisherman cried, 'I have found paradise.'

This was Udadost, the land of sprites and fairies, where otherworldly creatures led the brave and the kind to good fortune. Before him was a little house with a mossy roof, and a cat curled up by the chimney.

86

'Welcome to Udrost, you must be exhausted and hungry after ug for a feast! The fisherman followed his cottage.

He was astonished to discover that inside was like a palace. There was a table heaped fish, fruit

journey. Please join the old man into

With fresh bread and cheese, cakes and cider.

'Tuck in,' the old man said 'soon my sons will be here, and they'll join us. You just passed them out on the sea.'

'I saw no men, only three cormorants,' the fisherman replied. The old man chuckled. 'Those were my sons! They're out at sea, searching for the brave and kind!'

87

The fisherman was ravenous and he ate and ate but no matter how much he put away the platters and pitchers remained full to the brim. When he finally gave up and pushed away his plate, the door opened and three lads swept in.

'Come on,' they said warmly, 'let's go fishing!'

The fisherman really didn't want to get back out on the water, but he was too polite to argue with his generous hosts.

So, they went to sea and caught fish after fish and soon the boat was overloaded with their catch. 'We'll go out again tomorrow,' the lads said as they travelled back. And that's what they did every day for a month.

88

The fisherman loved his life of plenty. But he missed his family, so, at last he told the old man he must go home. The old man agreed.

'Come again before Christmas though, we'll go fishing and you can sell your catch.' The fisherman promised he'd be back and the old man gave him a large boat fitted with new sails.

And he filled it with everything the fisherman could want, both for his journey home and presents for his loved ones, and, of course, lots of fish.

'Whenever you wish to return, follow the flight of the cormorants and you'll find us.' the old man said.

When the Fisherman arrived home, his family were overjoyed.
But when his greedy Neighbor saw all his goods, he was
desperate to find out the Fisherman's secret. The Fisherman
saw no need to keep his good
luck to himself and told
his neighbour all about
Vørøst.

'I want to visit
this place!' the
neighbour said.
'Watch for the
cormorants then',
the fisherman replied

'You must follow them,
but remember, they
only help the brave and
the kind to good fortune!'
'Yes, yes....' said the Neighbor as
he set out to sea.

When the fisherman
himself returned to
Vørøst, as
promised, he asked
about his neighbour
but the old man
just shook his
head. The fisherman
filled his boat,
sailed home
and sold so many fish, he became a
rich man. And his neighbor was never seen again.

90

Eighteen

The goats that kept Cordelia in milk, cheese, curds and company were not behaving. One in particular was behaving very badly. She'd escaped and was running up the lane towards Zed.

'Quick, grab her,' yelled Cordelia, but Zed was too late. The goat flicked her back legs and skipped to one side.

'They chewed through the rope!' shouted Cordelia. 'Now, whatever you do, don't let her get past you. And don't hesitate! You've got to pretend you're indifferent, get close and pin her to the wall.'

Zed looked at the goat.

'Don't make eye contact!' roared Cordelia.

Zed looked at the gnarled, pointy horns.

'And don't grab the horns. They break easier than you think.'

So Zed looked at the soft ears and the pale eyes, *oops, no, not the eyes*, just the ears, the soft pink, floppy ears–

'When she thinks you're no longer interested she'll come closer. Can't help it. Too bleedin' nosey! And then you can throw yourself at her. Grab her legs if you like.'

Like didn't really come into it.

The goat bounced a little nearer and stopped to nibble a dandelion that was growing up through a pothole in the road.

Zed took a step closer – and another one – and then leaped forwards and grabbed the goat from behind. It started kicking and bleating, which sounded a lot like a human screaming, but Zed held on. It kicked out again, but stumbled and Zed was able to get hold of both legs. It was doing a kind of bucking bronco handstand; then they were doing a wheelbarrow race up the lane.

'Don't let go!' yelled Cordelia and moving quicker than Zed thought possible, she was at the front end, throwing a rope over the goat's head and tugging sharply. She pulled an apple out of her pocket, gave it to the runaway and leaned against the wall to get her breath.

'Good work, Zed!' she gasped.

Cordelia got out the remains of Zed's birthday cake and placed it before her on the table.

'Ha – a scapegoat!' she said, chuckling as she bustled around the kitchen. 'Very biblical!'

'Huh?'

'An *escaped goat* – a scapegoat?'

Zed still looked blank.

'Don't you know what a scapegoat is, child? Someone who is blamed for the sins of others?'

'Well, yes,' said Zed.

'It was Sennan who gnawed through the tether, but it was Moppet who got a proper whack from me because I was already cross and then she trod on my toe! That's why she charged through the hedge and off into the wilderness – well up the lane, anyway.'

Zed nodded and looked longingly at the last slice of cake on the plate.

'Go on. Take it.'

'I've brought you some more rubber bands,' said Zed, knowing that Cordelia used them to secure the rounds of coloured cloth she put on the top of her jam jars. She fumbled with the popper on her dungarees and scooped out the contents of her pocket.

Cordelia stopped, dead still. Then she leaned in towards the table, screwing up her eyes, and reached out to pick up the leather bracelet. The one Zed had found on the floor of the boathouse. She held it up close to her face and turned it around, then placing it in one palm she gently bounced her hand up and down as if to try the weight of it. As if to check that it was real.

'Oh my,' she said quietly. Her hand trembled and she dropped clumsily onto a chair. All the colour had faded from her cheeks.

'Cordelia?' said Zed, 'Cordelia, what's the matter?'

'I – I'm sorry. Where did you find it?'

'The bracelet?' said Zed. 'I found it in the boathouse.'

'That's not a bracelet, child. It's a snare.'

'A snare?'

'Gawen's snare. The one he used to fish with.' She carefully placed it back on the table. 'It's the one he made for the cormorant.'

Nineteen

So that was it. The boathouse was a crime scene.

Man had waged war on these birds before, but Gawen's betrayal was different; it was personal. He'd befriended the cormorant, named her, lived with her and worked with her. She trusted him and then died at his hands.

Zed lay on her bed staring up at the beams. Her thoughts sliding around like a tile puzzle: all the pieces were interlinked, but they had to be shifted up and down and from side to side, arranged and re-arranged. She definitely needed some help.

When Zed pushed open the door to Amy's room, there was a strange smell, sweet and sweaty, like Mum's bamboo socks when they burnt on the Aga.

Where did she get that then? Dad better not find out.

Amy was sprawled out on her bed. 'What's up?' she said, grinning like an idiot.

Suddenly Zed felt a bit light-headed. She pushed her sister's legs over and sat down on the end of the bed.

'You got a moment?'

'Ha – you're joking right? I'm struggling to choose from all the offers I've got tonight, parties to go to, films to see, bands–'

She was giggling like a five year old.

'Ames! This is serious.'

'Okay, okay,' she said, sitting up. 'Pass me that bottle of water and I'm all ears.'

'So, let me backtrack a bit here,' she said, ten minutes later, when Zed paused for breath. 'And I have to say, I'm loving this.' She rubbed her hands together, which wasn't that reassuring. 'You're genuinely convinced that we're under attack from a flock of vengeful cormorants?'

'Yes! And we're the scapegoats because we're the first humans who have dared to use the boathouse since Eve was killed. So we're the primary targets, but the more humans the birds can unsettle, the more lives they can upset, even destroy, the better.'

Amy was frowning now and nodding slowly. She was definitely struggling to concentrate. 'And you reckon it all started on the morning after the storm?'

'It must have been something to do with the bread left in the boathouse. I think the cormorants got at it somehow, before Dad handed out his samples all over town.'

'So, it's a kind of *blót*?'

'A what?'

'A *blót*. It's, like, a pagan thing. Luke's mate Zoph used to go off on these weekend festivals up near the Scottish Borders and they'd have these *blóts*. They'd do some kind of weird sacrifice. In the old days it would involve killing animals and drinking goblets of blood, but they ate crisps, vegan sausages and drank lots of beer, and then they'd ask for a blessing, you know, world peace, harmony with nature, all that stuff. 'Zoph was always trying to get us to go along but I'd never have got that one past Mum and Dad. Anyway I didn't much fancy it and luckily it wasn't really Luke's scene either.'

'Not dark enough?' Zed asked.

'Bit hippy for us,' said Amy. 'So, anyway,' she was on a roll now, 'it's like the cormorants did their own version, but in reverse. They sacrificed their own blood, which is why they were pecking the hell out of each other, but instead of a blessing they requested some kind of curse to be put on the bread – and anyone who ate it!'

Not bad for someone off their head.

'Yes!' said Zed. 'And maybe some ended up in the water and on the beaches, well you'd only need a seagull to get hold of one, and maybe the chef at Clewmor Hall sneezed while he was eating his and little particles of bread ended up floating about in the air – sounds ridiculous, but who knows? The last two rolls were definitely eaten by Mum and Dad just before their row!'

'You saw the cormorants at the boathouse. And you said one landed on the slip just before Mum fell.'

'Denzil said they never forget.'

'Obviously not.'

'And that it was my job to make peace.'

'Well, it sounds like they mean business. So you'd better get on with it!'

'It's kind of easier said than done!' Zed replied.

Amy got up off her bed, walked over to her dressing table, picked up a cup of cold tea and gulped it down. Then she turned and said, 'Okay, so just assuming for a moment that you haven't completely lost the plot, then it's a misunderstanding, right?'

'Huh?'

She started walking in circles around the room.

'Gawen didn't kill the bird out of malice or greed. Yes, cormorants have often been treated badly by mankind, but *he* didn't want a shilling in return for Eve's head, *he* didn't kill her because she'd served her purpose, or got old and slow–'

'No, he neglected her because he was grieving for his dead girlfriend.'

'And didn't the fact that he drank himself to death prove how miserable he was?'

'Exactly! They were both victims of the same tragedy!'

'Well, if you can find a way to explain that to the cormorants, then maybe, just maybe, they'll re-think.'

They looked up animal communication on the internet and found quite a bit of information on talking to non-humans, once they'd got past all the Dr Doolittle stuff, and much to Zed's surprise there were whole websites dedicated to communicating with horses, dogs and cats. There was nothing specifically on birds though, that would have been too much to hope for.

It seemed that animals were masters of intuitive communication and all you needed to do was engage in telepathy. Apparently, you could send a feeling simply by experiencing it and imagining it travelling. And you just opened yourself up to hear their response.

'It makes it all sound so easy,' Zed groaned, throwing herself back onto Amy's pillows. 'But I need to make them understand specific, complicated stuff, not ask if their left paw is hurting.'

'Well, there's no way this is going to work anyway,' said Amy. 'Didn't you read the first paragraph? It says the most important factor is mutual trust!'

Zed stood up, stretched and walked over to the empty chest of drawers. She peered at herself in the mirror, sucked in her cheeks and started squeezing the spots on her nose.

Amy googled *cormorant* and found a restaurant in Norfolk. It had two lousy reviews.

'You need some sort of medium,' she said.

'What's that?'

'You know, like one of those people you go and see when you want to engage with the spirit world. They're a kind of go-between.'

Oddly enough, Zed hadn't felt much need to *engage with the spirit world* so this was way off her radar.

'So what you're saying is, I need some kind of half-human half-bird type person, who will go and have a chat with the cormorants.'

'Yeah, that would be good,' said Amy.

'I'll put an advert in the Cornish Guardian,' said Zed, sitting back down. 'I'm sure the responses will come flying in.'

'Ha – I see what you did there,' said Amy with a wry smile. 'Flying in. Very good.'

But Zed wasn't listening. She'd had a thought.

Rather a good one, actually.

She picked up Amy's phone. 'Denzil said something about – ah, here we go.' She bounced up and down on the bed.

'I've got it Ames, we need Kerra!'

'Kerra?'

'Yeah, the one who was going to marry Gawen.'

'Well, she's going to know what happened, sure, but why would they listen to her?'

'Because she drowned! Here, listen to this: *According to Norwegian myth, people who die at sea can visit their former homes in the shape of a cormorant.*'

'Okaay,' said Amy.

'Well, if we can find a way to reach her ghost or spirit, or whatever, maybe write her a letter, or–'

'Write her a letter?'

'Look, I know it sounds a bit weird,' said Zed.

'You're telling me!'

'Well, I don't know, but if we can get hold of her somehow, then she can take on the form of a cormorant and explain to them how it really was, not as one of the enemy, but as one of them.'

'And she can apologise on behalf of her boyfriend – and I suppose all humankind while she's at it?'

'Okay, okay, it's stupid, right?'

'The letter bit is, for sure. Maybe we should get that guy involved. He sounds like he knows his stuff.'

'Denzil?'

'Why not?'

'Nah – he basically said it was my problem and I should get it fixed.'

'Yeah, but–'

'And anyway, if it came to it and he had to choose between us and the cormorants, I'm pretty sure he'd choose the cormorants. Every time.'

'Well, that only leaves us one option then. A séance!'

'Oh jeez, really?' said Zed with a groan.

'Yep!'

'And I suppose you want to get Luke involved too.'

Amy shrugged. 'We don't need Luke,' she said. 'He's taught me all he knows!'

They started making a list.

'Okay, so we'll need candles, new ones, without any kind of history, and incense,' said Amy. 'I think we should go for sandalwood as that's good for lifting the vibrations of the space.'

Zed rolled her eyes.

'You've got to get into it, otherwise we don't stand a chance.'

Yeah, whatever.

'We'll need some warm salt water, to cleanse the summoning space–'

'Summoning space? Are you for real?'

'Yes! Summoning space! The place where we do it. It needs to be somewhere we're not going to be disturbed by Mum or Dad. And the best place is somewhere that she has a history. I think we should go down to the boathouse.'

'No way!' said Zed.

Amy looked at her. 'Okay, well, maybe one of the outbuildings or something. She probably went there at some point. We'll use a shot glass instead of a planchette, Luke always said they work better and, of course, we'll need a Ouija board.'

'Like the ones in the crystal shop?'

'Exactly. We'll go and have a look first thing in the morning and then do it tomorrow night.'

Zed did not like the sound of this, but then she didn't much like the sound of any of it.

'That seems... very soon.'

'From what you've told me, I don't think we can waste any time.'

Zed needed a bit of headspace, a bit of time to de-freak.

'Well, let me sleep on it.'

'Ha – you'll be lucky!' Amy grinned. 'Oh, and no caffeine or dairy. In fact, give breakfast a miss. It's best just to eat fruit and veg the day before.'

'No breakfast?' Zed was horrified. 'Are you having a laugh?'

'You can have, like, an apple or something – for lunch.'

'One flippin' apple?'

'Zed, we've got serious work to do,' said Amy. 'And you've got to keep a clear state of mind!'

That was rich coming from her!

Twenty

When they arrived at Clewmor Crystals the following morning, they found the sandalwood incense and a box of tea lights. The Ouija boards were no longer on display in the middle of the shop, but there were two tucked away on a shelf at the back, and as soon as Amy picked one up the shopkeeper silently brought out another two from the storeroom and propped them up against a display of books. He then hovered behind them, humming tunelessly to himself while Zed and Amy tried to make up their minds. Even the cheapest was nearly thirty quid. Zed worked hard for her allowance and had a list as long as her arm of things she would rather spend it on.

'Forget about the money, I'll split it with you,' said Amy. 'Which one are you drawn to?'

Zed looked the boards. They were all laid out in the same way. In the top left-hand corner was a YES, with a picture of a sun, and in the top right-hand corner was a NO, with a picture of a moon. Then the bottom left said HELLO, and the bottom right said GOODBYE. All the letters of the alphabet were spread in an arc across the middle of the board and the numbers 0-9 were written out below. The most expensive board was a highly varnished cross section of a tree, with the letters carved and singed into the wood and the cheapest was made of shiny plastic with big, red gothic writing.

'Define *drawn to*,' said Zed.

'Can you feel a resonance? Do any make you tingle?'

'I'm feeling a kind of tingle, well more of a rumble actually. In my tummy!' hissed Zed.

Amy kicked her.

'Can't we just make one?' Zed asked. 'It would be so much cheaper.'

The shopkeeper, sensing his sale slipping away, went back to the till and picked up his book on divination.

'It needs to be varnished,' said Amy, 'so that things can slide easily over the surface.'

'Well, couldn't we make our own letters and stuff, and lay them out under that piece of glass that's up in the stable?'

'I s'pose so!' said Amy.

'And then we can design something that is really personal to Kerra, something that encourages her to come to us, maybe.'

Zed wandered over to the crystals. She put her hand into a plastic box filled with little chunks of green stone.

Peridot – *good for those undergoing traumatic emotional situations.*

Well, if you were going to buy into all of this then one of those would be a better use of their cash! Or even better:

Kunzite – *helpful for anxiety and panic attacks. This crystal can create a protective shield around the body.*

And then she saw

Blue Tourmaline – *aids communication with a higher realm.*

It was a lovely smoky colour.

'Let's get a bit of this too,' she said to Amy. 'Like a present or something, you know, for Kerra.'

'I got it,' said Amy, marching over to the till to pay.

Zed's phone pinged. She yanked it out of her pocket. Maybe it was Bethany and about time – but it was a missed call from Dad.

Another crystal caught Zed's eye:

Rose Quartz – *helps release lingering emotional baggage.*

'Get me out of here!' she said, heading for the door.

Zed wondered if they could spend the money they'd saved on a donut – or maybe an apple turnover or one of those iced whirls with a cherry on top.

'You know what?' Amy whispered as they stepped down onto the pavement, accompanied by a tinkling of bells. 'Luke always said that the energy came from the people present, not the board itself!'

'I'll be lucky if I've got any energy at all,' Zed muttered.

Mum was sitting on the back step when they got home, half way through another bottle of wine and staring at the willows down by the stream.

'Where's Dad?' asked Zed.

'He's gone away for a few days,' she said in a frail voice.

'Why?' Zed asked.

'Well, that's sodding brilliant!' said Amy, not waiting for an answer. 'He dumps us here, and then when things don't go quite how he planned them; he runs away?'

'He's not running away,' said Mum. 'I suggested he go to see Granny Steph. It will give him a chance to think all this through.'

'Think it through?' said Zed. 'You *are* joking, right? We're already here! Surely the *thinking it through* bit happened way back?'

'Not the move. I meant, him and me, I figured we could all do with a bit of space.'

'Space?' yelled Amy. '*Space?* We've got too much bloody space! Isn't that why he wanted us to come here?'

'There are lots of reasons we're here,' said Mum.

'Really?' shouted Amy. 'Well, you know what I think? Yeah, you like it here, but you also like East Sussex! We could have moved there, but eighty miles might not have done it. It might not have been enough distance between me and Luke, and Dad had to be sure, didn't he?'

'It wasn't just about that, Amy, and you know it,' said Mum.

'Oh, but you admit now that it was partly about that? At last! Get you on your own and at last some bloody honesty! Well, I guess that's progress.' Amy pushed past and went into the house.

Mum slowly lifted her glass towards her lips, but her hand was shaking so much she returned it to the step with a clunk.

'Are you okay?' said Zed.

'Just a bit – my arm's painful,' she said, rolling up her sleeve.

The scabs were weeping thick yellow gunk and the whole limb was red and inflamed.

'Mum, that really doesn't look good.'

She sighed and her eyes filled with tears.

'What's happening to us, Zed?'

Amy had an old cork notice board and they carried it up to the stable, along with paper, pens and a set of watercolour paints. While Zed wrote out the letters and the numbers, Amy painted a bright yellow sun and a pale blue moon. Zed tried to remember everything Cordelia had told her about Kerra, but it wasn't much, so she drew blackberries and fish, the boathouse and a fiddle. She drew a young couple perched by the river and a cormorant with its wings stretched out, sitting on the stern of a fishing boat. She tried to channel Denzil's fascination and affection for the birds, rather than her own fear and distrust, and it came out okay.

They found three logs of a similar height in the wood store and put them in the middle of the floor, placed the board on the top and arranged all the letters, numbers and the pictures around the edge. Zed cleaned the glass with soapy water, newspaper and vinegar, and laid it on top. Then she found two more stumpy logs for them to sit on. Amy stood back and leaned against the doorframe.

'The light should be behind us, so let's put two tea lights up there,' she said, pointing to a low shelf attached to the left wall, 'and another couple on there,' she said, nodding towards an overturned feeding trough. 'Leave the incense and matches by the door and we'll come back when it's dark. Now take a walk and listen to some music or something. Basically, you need to hang out by yourself.'

Like that is going to be a challenge!

Twenty One

It started to get dark around nine thirty.

Zed had told Mum that both she and Amy weren't feeling great and didn't want any supper. She'd been prepared to give details about stomach cramps, diarrhoea and a bug going around Clewmor, but Mum had just nodded and said she wasn't hungry either. She'd kissed the top of Zed's head and hobbled up the stairs to her room.

Amy boiled a kettle and made a salt solution. While that was cooling down in a jam jar on the patio, they sat in silence and watched the moths throw themselves at the light in the roof of the veranda.

Eventually Amy spoke.

'If you're wearing any jewellery, take it off. The same goes for a watch.'

'I'm not,' said Zed.

'Are you scared?'

'Yep.'

'Fair enough, but try not to be too jumpy, it puts them off.'

'Them? We only want to speak to one of um – them, don't we?'

Amy shrugged. 'Yeah, that's all very well, but you never know who's going to turn up. Anyone might want to make contact and we have to be willing to talk to them.'

'But only someone who died at sea can return as a cormorant.'

'I get that, and I get why we need to speak to Kerra, but think of it like a telephone. If we get a phone and switch it on, and it has a charged up battery and good signal, then just when we're ready to ring someone, someone might give *us* a ring. And it might be a wrong number or a cold call from Mumbai, but we'd still probably answer, wouldn't we? Even if it's only to say we're not who they want, or we don't want what they're selling.'

'How many times have you done this?'

'A few.'

'And did it work?'

'It's hard to say. Most of the time we were pretty trashed and there were a lot of hands on the glass, so who knows if someone else was pushing it for a laugh. It definitely moved though. And it definitely spelled out some stuff.'

Zed felt her back go cold. She tried not to think about going to see Cordelia for a hot chocolate, or reading her book, or making some origami, or calling Beth, or how much she'd rather do almost anything other than what they were planning.

'Come on then,' said Amy. 'Let's get to it.'

Amy used the torch on her phone to light their way up to the stable. When they got there, she turned the phone off and left it on the window ledge outside. There was just enough moonlight coming through the top of the stable door for them to see the matches and light the little candles. Then they shut themselves inside.

It was very dark to begin with and not being able to see much, the damp smell of hay and rotting wood intensified, along with the sound of their shallow breathing, but her eyes adjusted as the tea lights flickered, then settled into a steady glow: the flames taking hold, blackening the wick and turning the opaque wax to liquid. The shadow of a garden fork, propped up against the feeding trough, took shape across the room, its blurred prongs like elongated tombstones.

Amy sprinkled some of the salt solution around the floor and then used the rest to wipe over the glass of the Ouija board. She lit the incense cones and sat down on one of the wooden logs by their makeshift table. The spicy richness of the sandalwood blended with the earthy smell of the straw creating a thick, heady, soothing aroma. Amy peered up at Zed, who was still standing by the door, and without taking her eyes off her sister she pulled out a small glass tumbler from her bag and placed it, rim down, in the middle of the board. It was time to begin.

Zed took a deep breath and stepped forward into the darkness, immediately realising how reassuring it had been to have her back pressed up against the wall. Sitting in the middle of the room, anything could creep up behind her.

'What the– ?' She leaped off the stool. It was an owl, hooting from the tree just outside.

'Try and relax,' said Amy, her voice quiet and low. 'You need to be calm but responsive,' she continued. 'Don't push the glass, but allow it to move if you feel it wants to.'

'What if it's someone evil?'

'If we need to, we'll politely ask the spirit to leave.'

'What if they try to, well – to hurt us?'

'Imagine yourself bathed in a protective light. And stay positive. We want to do good here and so should only attract good energy.'

'Mmm – I don't buy that,' said Zed. 'We've attracted plenty of energy around here already and it's definitely not very friendly!'

'Shh...'

Amy shut her eyes and gently rocked herself from side to side. Finally, she spoke, 'In this sacred space we call upon our friend Kerra. We know of the love you felt for Gawen. We've heard of your warmth and kindness and in that spirit, we ask for your help. We respectfully request that you speak to us though this Ouija board.'

The light flickered and the owl hooted again.

'Please indicate your presence here by moving the glass to *Yes*.'

Zed held her breath until she felt light-headed. Her fingers were trembling on the glass, but the tremble was definitely hers. They waited. Nothing.

Amy spoke again.

'Please let us know you're here with us. Please give us a sign.'

Was that–?

And she heard it again – not an owl this time, but a scrabbling, a scratching close by. Very close by.

Amy jumped up and the glass jerked forward.

Zed let out a yelp.

'Shh...' said Amy, sitting back down. Her eyes were shut again. 'Kerra, is that you?'

The scratching continued. It was coming from the hay bale.

'If you are with us, please move the glass to *Yes*.'

Again they waited.

Zed could feel her blood surging through her wrists and into her hands. All the tension in her body seemed focused on her fingertips; they were throbbing against the cool glass, but still nothing happened.

'It's – it's a mouse!' whispered Zed.

'It's a sign!' said Amy. 'Concentrate!'

'It's just a mouse,' said Zed again.

And they waited.

And they waited.

Zed's hand began to ache. It was hard not to drop her elbows onto the board.

'We're waiting for a sign,' said Amy, her voice a little more shill.

And still they waited.

In silence.

Until the first tea light spluttered and went out. It was followed by two more in quick succession.

104

'Is there anybody there? Anybody?' asked Amy suddenly.

Zed peered at her sister.

What was she playing at? That wasn't the deal. They weren't looking for *anybody*, they were looking for Kerra.

'I'm cold,' said Zed.

And then the last candle died too, plunging them into complete darkness.

'And hungry.'

'Are you there?' said Amy frantically. 'Please–'

And then Zed heard a sob.

'Ames? Ames, is that you?'

And then a sort of moaning.

'Amy?' Zed took her hands off the glass and reached across the board, fumbling for her sister's fingers.

'Amy!' she hissed urgently. 'Answer me.'

'I'm here,' Amy whimpered and then, 'I've had enough. Let's go.'

They stood up, awkwardly holding onto each other, and Zed knocked over the board with her knees. Not that it mattered now. Stepping backwards she kept her hands on Amy's shoulders and guided her, as best she could, around the logs and together they groped their way to the door. It seemed to take forever for Zed to find the phone, turn it on and slide the screen up to activate the torch, but as soon as the dull yellow light illuminated the steps, Amy broke away and ran, wailing, down to the house.

And Zed didn't hang around either.

Twenty Two

Zed assumed Amy would go straight upstairs, but instead she was waiting for her in the sitting room. She'd turned on the standard lamp and was huddled up in the corner of the sofa, under a pile of cushions. Her eyeliner had run onto her cheeks and then been dragged into thick black smears. Zed could see from the dark streaks on her wrists that she'd been trying to clean herself up.

'I was glad when you wanted to make your own board, you know, personalise it, 'cause I thought I wouldn't be tempted again. This time it would just be about Kerra.'

Zed sat down at the other end of the sofa. She angled her body to face her sister.

'I don't really understand. Tempted by what?'

Amy didn't look at Zed, but held out a small square of flimsy paper. It looked like a photograph, grainy and nearly all black. There was some writing along the bottom: a date and time.

Zed had no idea what it was supposed to be. In the middle of the black was a kidney shaped smudge of grey.

'You still don't know, do you?'

'Know what?'

'That I was pregnant.'

Zed didn't know, and her first thought was that she didn't want to know. Not even now.

'When?' she said eventually.

'At the beginning of the year. Do you remember when I was being sick all the time? When you thought I was bulimic?'

Zed remembered all those mornings before school when Amy wouldn't let anyone into the bathroom.

'I did a test, and it was positive, so Mum took me for a scan. That's it.' She waved at the bit of paper in Zed's hand. 'Eight weeks.'

'What did they say?'

'Who? Mum and Dad?'

'Yeah.'

'Well, Mum was as shaken up as me, and just sad, really sad, like it was all her fault. And Dad was away, and we were going to tell him when he got back, but I started bleeding and it was, like, really bad cramps – and then – not long after we had proof there was a problem, it was no longer a problem.'

'You – lost it?'

'Yep. It died. Because I didn't want it. I think it knew.'

'Well, maybe–'

'Don't say it, Zed. Don't say what they said. You see, only Luke wanted it. He was the only one. And he was really happy when I told him. For the three days that we thought I was going to have a baby he was the happiest I've ever seen him. I was shocked and terrified, but he was, like – it was like all the crap in his family faded away because he was going to do it right. He wanted us to move in together.'

'I remember that bit.'

'I was so stunned because we were careful and–'

'I bet Dad was furious.'

'Well, by the time Mum told him, it didn't matter. I mean he was furious anyway, obviously, but he knew he wasn't going to have to convince me to get rid of it. By the time he knew, there were no decisions to be made.'

Zed stared at the photograph.

An actual niece or nephew.

'And I think that was when he really took a turn against Luke. Not because of everything that he is, but because he would have wanted me to give up school and have a baby – because he wanted me to keep it.'

'So I'm guessing Luke was pretty cut up.'

'He was devastated. He wouldn't stop crying and then, when it all calmed down a bit, I think he actually wanted us to try and get pregnant again!' Amy slammed her hand over her mouth and for a moment Zed thought she was going to be sick, but it was muffling a giggle. Her eyes immediately welled up again.

'Can you imagine?'

Zed really couldn't. She couldn't imagine any of this. Ever. She didn't want to try imagining any of this.

'So, do you see now, why Dad wanted to get me away from him? Why he thought it was so urgent to drag us down here?'

'Yes,' said Zed. 'Yes, I guess that makes sense.' After a moment she added, 'But it was also for Mum, well, I mean it was for them, wasn't it? Something pretty big had to change, right?'

'Yeah of course. Especially after she, you know.'

Zed nodded.

'And they said they felt guilty 'cause they weren't there for me and that wasn't going to help Mum was it? She and Dad had a screaming match that ended up with them both in tears, then they sat me down and said it was their fault for not making me feel loved enough and special enough.'

'Sounds nauseating.'

Yeah, it really was! And they said that they'd taken their eye off the ball and spent too much time dealing with their own issues and it was because *they'd failed me* that I found all Luke's attention, and *adoration* was the word Dad used, so compelling.'

'Ouch.'

'Well, you can imagine how that went down. Basically, Dad was saying that the one thing that was mine, me and Luke, wasn't really about me and Luke at all, it was all about them!'

Amy shook her head and started chewing at her nail. 'So, you think this move is nothing to do with you, but from where I'm sitting, it's as much about you as anyone else. They want to make sure you don't mess up like I did.'

As if.

'They want to be here for you. Dad wants to be in the same building as us, for more than just a couple of nights a week. And, yeah, Mum has always been here physically I guess, but she wants to be present you know, happy and with it enough for it to mean something, like she's actually in the room!'

'Sounds like a good idea,' said Zed, 'but it's not really working out that way is it?'

'No,' sighed Amy. 'Right now, it's not looking good.'

So many questions were going round in Zed's head, but she wasn't sure she wanted to ask them. Or if it would be okay to do so, but this one, she kept coming back to.

'Why didn't anyone tell me?'

'About the baby?'

Zed nodded.

'I didn't want them to. In fact, I told them not to tell you.'

'I don't understand.'

'Look, I had Luke. I *only* had Luke and this was about us. I didn't tell anyone else as I guess I didn't have anyone else to tell. I knew if you knew though, you wouldn't keep it a secret. You would tell your friends. I don't exactly blame you for that, maybe I was even jealous that you had those friends to tell, but I couldn't bear the idea of you all sitting round discussing it, being all superior and like, *look at how Amy is screwing up her life.*'

There was no point protesting. Even as Amy was talking Zed was wondering what they'd make of it, when she messaged them. How much Kab would enjoy it. She looked at Amy, all twisted up at the end of the sofa and it stopped her in her tracks. Like properly stopped her. A full on slamming of the brakes.

'And anyway, because Luke was into all that stuff,' Amy said, 'we did the Ouija board with this.' She reached for the scan photo. 'I just felt so bad that it wasn't wanted. So sad. It was mine to look after and I just flushed it away down the toilet. Literally. I guess I – I think I felt really guilty and I just wanted to say sorry. I still really want to – say sorry.'

She swallowed and clenched her jaw, and once again, inky tears trailed down her cheeks.

And Zed nodded.

It was the best she could do.

Twenty Three

Dad rang the following morning. He sounded a bit too chirpy when he said he was helping out Granny Steph until the weekend. When Zed told him that Mum was really struggling and that she needed him more than Granny Steph did, he gave up the act. He said that they'd talked for over an hour the night before and Mum had told him in no uncertain terms to stay where he was.

'She's pretty sure that's what she wants,' he said.

'But why?' asked Zed.

'I'm not the easiest person to live with and–'

'What about your bread business?'

'The bakery isn't going anywhere.'

'But – what about all the people who liked your bread? The ones who wanted more?'

'I've given some of them a call, no one wants to commit to a regular order at the moment. What with the hotel shutting down, and maybe it's the economy, or the weather, or all that rubbish washing up on the beaches, but the tourist trade has taken a real hammering. Even those with holiday homes are choosing to stay away.'

'We're running out of food!'

'Granny's done you an internet order.'

'Seriously?'

'She's discovered online shopping. Big time!'

'And they'll deliver down here?'

'It's going to arrive tomorrow, apparently.'

'There'll be square bread in plastic, Dad.'

'Yuck!' He said it with a chuckle, but she could still hear the sadness in his voice.

'Is Amy around?'

Zed walked up the stairs and knocked on her sister's door. There was no reply.

'Best not to wake her,' said Dad and Zed wasn't going to argue.

'Speak later then?'

He seemed reluctant to put down the phone.

'Got to go, Dad.'

'Look after Mum, won't you?'

'I will.'

'And–'

'And what, Dad?'

'I miss you guys.'

An hour or so later, Zed went upstairs to take Mum a cup of tea and a blackening banana. She found her half sitting, half lying in bed, boiling hot and mumbling about eggshell paint, pheasants and toothpaste. When Zed asked her what was wrong, she couldn't seem to focus. She leaned forwards, tried to speak and collapsed back onto her sodden pillow.

'Mum!' Zed shook her. 'Mum! Have you taken something?'

Zed yelled for Amy, but there was no answer.

'Mum?' Zed looked at the bedside table, ran her hand around the side of the pillows and under the duvet, she got down on her hands and looked on the floor and under the bed. There was one packet of Paracetamol, but only two pills were missing.

'Mum?'

'My arm–'

Zed grabbed the phone and rang 999.

While they were waiting for the paramedics Zed got warm water, like she'd learned in her First Aid course at school, and sponged Mum's forehead and hair. She could feel the heat radiating from her injured arm.

Mum kept trying to apologise and say Zed shouldn't worry.

Yeah, right.

A yellow and green car pulled up outside and Zed ran out to meet the driver, who introduced himself as Dave. He followed her up to the bedroom, took one look at Mum's arm, popped a thermometer in her ear and said,

'You'd better pack her a bag. She's dehydrated and she's probably going to need some strong IV antibiotics.'

He got straight on the phone.

'And how did she do this?' he asked.

'I slipped, down by the boathouse in the woods,' Mum replied, slurring her words.

'Well, I'm very glad you called us when you did. It's a really nasty infection. To be honest, I've not seen anything like it, not from an injury like that. She's not diabetic, is she?'

'Nope,' said Zed.

'Is there any other history I should be aware of, Mrs Root? Any issues with your immune system?'

Mum shook her head as firmly as she could.

'Is it definitely an infection?' asked Zed.

'Looks that way, but they'll have to run some tests.'

'Is there any chance she could – that she might have taken something?' Zed whispered.

Dave stopped for a moment and looked at Zed. Then he looked at Mum.

'Lucy? Are you with us? I need to ask you some questions.'

'Only arnica – I promise,' said Mum quietly.

'Who else is around?' asked Dave.

'Our neighbour across the road,' said Zed. 'And my older sister. She's still asleep.'

'Do you want to wake her up?'

'No, don't do that,' whispered Mum. 'She'll only make a fuss about Dad not being here and I'm not sure I can cope with that just now.'

'Where is he?' said Dave.

'He's on his way back,' Zed quickly replied.

It took a while for the ambulance to arrive, but when two more paramedics joined Dave, they helped Mum sit up and swing her legs down to the floor and then they lifted her into a little wheelchair, which they carried carefully down the stairs. Zed followed with her bag.

'You coming or staying put?' Dave asked her.

'She'll stay,' said Mum weakly.

'Really?' said Zed.

'Really, pet. I'll call you in a bit.'

'You can ring this number in an hour or so and you'll get an update,' said Dave, handing her a bit of paper. 'She'll be in good hands.'

Cordelia came out and stood with Zed while the ambulance pulled away up the lane. Zed quickly explained what had happened, then went inside to call Dad.

She picked up her phone from the windowsill and there was a message from Amy:

Feeling sad gone to see Luke.

She ran up the stairs and barged into Amy's room.

Duh! Of course she wasn't there. And neither was her phone, her bag or her coat.

Twenty Four

Zed couldn't get hold of Dad, so she left a message on his mobile. She gave him the number of the hospital and told him to hurry up and get going. She called Granny Steph, but she wasn't answering either. She didn't really know what to say to Amy and composed and deleted several messages before simply asking her to call back ASAP.

She paced around the house. She lay on her bed, but as soon as she was horizontal, she felt the familiar sizzling heat on her face and neck. She curled herself into a ball and lay there panting before forcing herself upright again and putting her head between her knees. Then she waited for her heartbeat to slow down and retreat back behind her ribs where it belonged.

It took a while.

She got up and walked stiffly down the stairs. After starving herself the day before, she realised she was actually pretty hungry. She looked in the fridge and took the last bit of Parmesan, which was basically rind, and she found some dried apricots in the larder. She walked down to the stream and ate her pathetic picnic sitting on the little bridge.

She looked at her phone, even though she knew she was too far from the Wi-fi. Beth hadn't contacted her for three days. She scrolled through all the messages she'd received since she'd been here – and there weren't that many. Beth was active enough on social media, she popped up on group chats all the time and she was posting pictures on a pretty regular basis.

Zed shut her eyes for a moment and tried to imagine Beth sitting next to her on the bridge. She pieced her together, like the puzzle postcard she'd sent her, starting with her hair, then her dimples, then her mouth, the funny the way it parted when she did that lopsided grin. Then she thought of her hands, of them holding hands over the table in the café on the day she left and Beth saying they had one night left. What had she meant by that?

What did I want her to mean? Oh, god...

Zed thrust herself forward so that her feet were fully submerged in the cold water. She kicked them up and down, spraying herself.

Mum was really ill. Mum and Dad weren't good again and Amy was obviously all over the place. Dad's big dream was going down the pan.

If this was war, then the cormorants were winning.

And however hard she tried to think of an alternative, she kept coming back to Kerra. If there was any truth in the myth, then the way she died made her the perfect candidate to speak to the birds.

But how to reach her?

Zed didn't even know if she believed in ghosts, which wasn't a good start, but then a month back she wouldn't have believed that a bunch of estuary-dwelling birds would find a way to take revenge for a crime committed eighty years before. And ghost or no ghost, being separated from someone you loved was bad enough, add drowning to the mix and she wouldn't have been tempted to put in an appearance either. At least, not for two girls sitting in a stable, wafting incense about and scaring themselves senseless.

Zed looked at her phone.

Again.

She couldn't help it.

Any further help from Amy was obviously off the cards. She was probably somewhere on the motorway by now, listening to her grungy music and looking forward to a bittersweet reunion with Luke. He would whisper into her ear, his breath stale with nicotine and beer, and tell her that no one would ever love her as much as he did, and that they were destined to be together, that she was the only one who could take away his pain, and that if they could just have a baby – *Stop!*

She was doing it again.

And yeah, he *was* an idiot, but all things considered, maybe she should try giving the guy a break. After all, he was having a crap time too.

Cordelia was feeding scraps to the chickens and she waved as Zed came around the side of the house.

'How's your mother?'

'Oh, you know—'

'If I did, why would I be asking?'

'Well, when I called the hospital there wasn't any change really. They've done a lot of blood tests and got her on a drip, so I guess we'll have to wait and see.'

'Poor woman. Sounds ghastly!' said Cordelia. 'And what about you girls? Have you had lunch? Why don't you make yourselves an omelette?' She bent down to her wooden display case and picked up a box of eggs.

Zed took them reluctantly. She felt bad that Dad wasn't keeping up his end of the bargain. Cordelia was always giving them eggs and jam and half of her yeast starter, but she hadn't had any homemade bread for days.

'You know my dad's gone away, for a bit, don't you?' said Zed.

'Yes, but he'll be back soon, won't he?' said Cordelia. 'Are you minding the yeast starter?'

'Um, Dad was doing it twice a day I think, but then he put it in the fridge a while back.'

'That's fine. You can revive it when you need to, but you'll still to feed it once a week. Come on, get me some flour and a cup of water and I'll show you how.'

They went through the gate into Zed's garden. On the way Cordelia stooped down to pick up an apple that had rolled out of the box and onto the gravel. She held on to Zed's arm, to steady herself.

'Go on – it's bruised now. Throw it for Buttons.'

And Zed chucked the apple across the lawn, rather awkwardly, but it went a surprisingly long way.

Cordelia stood watching.

'Dum dum di dum– Come on, you can do it. Good boy. Now drop.'

Buttons did as he was told and was rewarded with another throw.

'Dum dum di dum– See? I knew I'd remember it eventually!' she said, turning to Zed.

'Mmm?'

Cordelia looked very pleased with herself. 'Last night, it came to me. Late it was, just before bed, and it came to me out of nowhere. And not just the tune, but the words too, all of them! And so I don't forget it again, I keep going over and over it. To make it stick.

> *You penned a song, wrote just for me,*
> *your voice was sweet and strong,*
> *you wrapped your arms around my waist,*
> *and kissed me all day long.'*

She sang it very low, tapping her hand on her thigh and when she'd finished, she looked at Zed. 'There's another two verses as well. Who would have thought it, eh? After all these years? I can't remember what I had for breakfast, but I've not forgotten a single word of that song!'

'Where's it from?' asked Zed. She had no idea what Cordelia was going on about, and frankly she had more important things to focus on.

'It's Kerra's song, you daft girl. The one I told you about! She used to sing it with Gawen, down by the boathouse. She sang it to me to get me to sleep – and that wasn't an easy task, apparently!'

Kerra's song. Of course!

'It's very pretty. Will you teach it to me?'

'Well, there's a thought. In case I do forget it again, eh?'

Zed smiled. *Something like that.*

Twenty Five

Zed made herself an omelette, as Cordelia had suggested, but it was more like scrambled eggs. In fact, it was more chopped up bits of pale yellow rubber, but she ate it anyway, out of the saucepan with a teaspoon, and then she went upstairs, got into bed and pulled her duvet over her head. She lay there, staring at the faint glow of light through the cotton and wadding, and tried not to think about how nice it felt to lie next to someone, instead of in a strange empty house all by herself. She pulled her phone out of her pocket and called Beth again, and she actually answered.

'Hey, you!'

'Oh, hi! You're there!' Zed quickly sat up and yanked her hair off her face.

'Yep. On my way out though–'

'Oh. I, um – I really like, need to talk to you.'

'Sure. Anytime. You know that.'

'Things are, well, lots of things have been happening.'

'Hang on a moment. Hey, you guys, wait up, I'm talking to Zed!'

'Who's there?'

'Oh, you know, the usual. They all say *hi*.'

'Right.'

'We're going to see a film at Liam's house. His parents are out this evening.'

'At Liam's house? What sort of film?'

'Give me a minute!' she yelled away from the phone, then came back. 'Hang on, I'm trying to find my other shoe.'

'What film are you watching?' Zed asked again.

'Well, I don't think Kab and Liam are going to be up for a rom com. Some sci-fi rubbish probably.'

'Ah, not this again! Not *all* sci-fi is rubbish. D'you remember that one–'

'Yeah, yeah – I know! Look I'd better be going.'

'Oh, okay. When's a good time?'

'For what?'

'To talk. To talk, like – properly.'

'Message me.'

'It's not the same.'

'Well, duh!'

'What does that mean?'

'You're five hours away Zed! Of course it's not the same. We'll speak soon though, yeah?' She blew two loud kisses – that was something – before she ended the call.

How could Beth think hanging out with Liam Marks might actually be an okay way to spend an evening? Even if everyone was going, it was still Liam's house! Which meant they'd have to engage with Liam's infantile sense of humour, his appalling taste in music – and probably films – and his feet that stank like rotting sewage.

Talking of which...

Zed got up off the bed. Maybe she didn't need to spend the evening alone after all.

'What time do you call this?' yelled Tamsin. She was standing down by the shore in a sporty looking turquoise bikini top and a wetsuit that was only pulled up as far as her waist. The neoprene arms flopped down to her knees, and looked pretty similar to the ribbons of rubbery black seaweed draped over the rock by the toilet block, some of which was tangled up with bits of blue rope and two rusty fishing rods. Just below the loos were three overflowing bins and a heap of rubbish that seemed totally out of proportion to the size of the beach – rusty cans, plastic bottles, crisp packets, an old kettle and a thigh-length wellington boot. Zed could see more rubbish strewn into clumps all the way down to the water and the smell hit her as soon as she stepped onto the sand. She tried not to breathe through her nose.

Tamsin was holding up what looked like an enormous bit of green cloth and trying to fold it into a manageable size. There were two other girls and a boy, who looked like they were finishing up and when Tamsin pointed up at Zed, they hugged her goodbye and set off up the beach.

'We've gotta go, but you okay to help her with the net?' said the boy as he walked past.

'Sure,' Zed replied to his back.

'Better late than never!' Tamsin swept her hair back with one hand while holding out the corner of the net to Zed with the other. Up close Zed could see the holes.

'I was aiming for fashionably late,' said Zed, but Tamsin obviously wasn't in the mood for banter.

'We meet at six,' she replied. 'But no worries. You're here now, that's what counts!'

Zed took the corner of the net and held it up as Tamsin stepped back and tried to shake it out. The stench was appalling.

What the hell?

She threw it down and stumbled backwards. It was filled with rotting dead fish.

'It's a gill net,' said Tamsin, trying not to laugh and picking up the corner again, now lying in the sand, and handing it back. 'The fish get half way in an' then the twine slips behind their gills, so they can't escape.' She tried shaking it out again. 'I should say, *was* a gill net. It's called a ghost net, when it's like this, discarded by a fisherman – an' this is the third one we've found this week.'

'It's disgusting,' said Zed.

'You're telling me. We're used to all the plastic, especially the bottles, but this is something else.'

'Are the bottles really that bad, usually I mean?'

'Are you having a laugh? Did you know there are, on average, a hundred an' fifty plastic bottles littering every mile of beach in the UK?'

'No, I didn't,' admitted Zed.

'Or that each one will be bobbing around in the marine environment for four hundred an' fifty years?'

'Nope. Didn't know that either.'

'So, you glug down a drink an' it takes, what two minutes? An' that's your legacy!'

'I meant are they usually a problem on this particular beach?'

'Well, it would be better if the shops didn't sell them in the first place, but at least most people use the recycling bins and the one or two left on the sand are picked up by one of us.' She looked around and shook her head. 'But something really strange is happening here, though, because all of this – it's way worse than normal.'

'It is pretty grim.'

'And a few bottles is one thing, but getting this net off the beach is gonna be a bit more of a challenge.'

'Maybe if we picked out the fish first?' suggested Zed.

Tamsin snorted, 'It's not funny. At all, but you should see your face!' Then she added, 'We did actually try that before you got here, but there are just too many and they're too – far gone. We've dragged it up enough though, so it won't get swept out again with the tide. I'll get my dad to come down with the four by four.'

Zed looked down. Even the water lapping at her flipflops had a bubbly beige scum. It definitely wasn't like this the last time she'd come here, the day she'd fallen flat on her face in the sand, the day she'd seen the cormorant.

'Come on,' said Tamsin. 'At least we can bag some of the stuff up at the top,' and she started striding up towards the road. Suddenly she squealed, grabbed her foot and dropped down onto the sand.

'Are you okay?' Zed ran over.

'No, I'm bloody not!' She was sitting cross-legged and rubbing her heel. Lying next to her on the sand was a little stripy plastic toy.

Can't have hurt that much!

And then Zed saw the three little hooks on the end.

'What's that?'

'A fishing lure. A pretty basic one – doesn't even look like a fish!'

Zed carefully picked it up between her thumb and finger and let it dangle, twinkling in the sun.

Tamsin put her hand out for Zed to pull her up and there was blood smeared all over her thumb and fingers. She wiped them off on the arm of her wetsuit.

'It doesn't make any sense,' she said, standing on one foot like a black flamingo. 'Lots of this, the nets, the rope and the tangled lines, in fact most of this is fishing stuff. What are they thinking? Why are they being so irresponsible? It's their livelihood they're threatening an' they're giving fishermen a bad name, with the locals, the holiday makers, the press.'

'Um – what *is* a fish lure?'

Tamsin looked at Zed and rolled her eyes. 'Does what it says on the tin.'

'Lures fish?'

She nodded. 'They're all colourful and flashy, bit like your sunglasses, Mr or Mrs Big Fish come along and says, 'I fancy a bit of that–'

'What's wrong with my sunglasses?'

'Nothing!' said Tamsin, chuckling. 'I can see myself in the mirrors, what's not to like?'

She cupped Zed's face in her hands, looked straight into the lenses and said, 'I fancy a bit of that!' and almost fell over again she found it so funny.

'Hey Tams, still at it?'

They both swung around and behind them at the top of the beach Zed saw two men with long hair, beards and matching denim jackets, shuffling towards them. They were swinging metal detectors.

'Hey, Joe,' Tamsin yelled back. 'Found anything?'

'At least *they're* happy,' she said to Zed with a wink. 'There's always some treasure to be found amongst the rubbish, right?'

'Been home for some tea,' Joe called back, 'but 'ad a very good afternoon, found a stash of old coins.'

120

'Three shillings!' said the other one.

'And they're old,' said Joe. 'Got the head of King George V on 'em!'

'Bit battered, but still worth something.'

'What year are your coins?' Zed asked casually, when they got close enough not to shout.

Joe thrust his hand into his pocket and pulled out a silver disc. He turned it over and held it up close to his face.

'Issued in 1911 by the looks of it.'

Zed nodded and stumbled.

Tamsin reached out to steady her. 'Are you alright?' she said. 'You've gone all sort of clammy.'

'Yes, it's – it's the smell I think,' said Zed. 'I'm sorry, I might have to go home.'

'Alright,' said Tamsin, gently patting Zed's back and looking really concerned. 'Wait, I'll walk with you, let me just grab my rucksack from over there.'

Zed staggered up the steps and onto the road.

While waiting for Tamsin she tried to concentrate on the lovely warm tingling up and down her spine and the calming rhythm of the waves – but all she could hear was Denzil's voice, throbbing in her ears.

In 1911, they 'ad a cull. A big one. An' those know-it-alls at County Hall offered a shilling for every cormorant head.

Twenty Six

Dad didn't come home that evening after all and the following morning Granny Steph called to say he was on a plane to Pisa – or was it Prague?

'Plymouth?' said Zed hopefully.

'All that travelling,' she moaned. 'I could never keep up.'

'But I only spoke to him yesterday,' said Zed. 'And he told me he was going to spend the next couple of days going through your shed.'

When he did call back, he was flapping. Big time.

'I didn't get your message until I landed!' he said. 'My old boss rang just after I spoke to you and I figured it wasn't doing me any good just moping around doing nothing. I thought I might as well earn some money and it's not as if we've got anything else coming in – but if I'd known, if I'd–'

'It's okay, Dad.'

'Yeah, well, I'm looking into flights and I'm coming straight home.'

'Won't that leave them in the lurch?'

'Yes, but–'

'Then stay. Mum's being looked after and I'll, um, we'll be fine.'

'But I should be there.'

'Dad. Do the job.'

'If anything changes, I'll be straight on that plane.'

'I know.'

Zed wandered into the garden, took off her dungarees and lay on the grass in the sun. While sweating the big stuff, she might as well do something about the colour of her legs! She had just got herself comfortable lying on her towel when she heard a voice, 'Hey Zed – you in?'

She grabbed the towel from under her bottom and tried to pull it over her, but it was too late.

'Why didn't you tell me about your Mum?'

Tamsin was standing on the gravel, the sun behind her, so that the outline of her head was all fuzzy like a halo. Zed squinted at her, tried to block out the light with one hand while using the other one to tug again at the towel.

'Hiya. And, um – sorry. I guess it just didn't come up.'

'Yeah right.'

'And it was sort of nice not to think about it for a bit.'

'And are *you* okay?'

'Me?'

'Yeah. I was a bit worried after you pulled that whitey on me!'

'I'm fine.'

'Good. I'm, um – glad. I was thinking about you all night.'

At least someone was.

'I came up this way to see if my brother was still hanging around.'

'I haven't been into the woods for a few days, I'm afraid.'

'I brought him some stuff, notebooks, pencils and things.'

'That's nice.'

'I didn't know if he'd be hungry.'

'Well, he looked in pretty good shape to me, not like the homeless we used to get round our way.'

'Yeah, well, he's into foraging – an' he's not actually homeless. Not really. He's got a mate he sometimes shacks up with downriver a bit, but he likes it, you know, being away from everything and everyone. It's his choice, his way of coping. What *are* you doing with that towel?'

'I'm trying to–'

'Why are you covering yourself up? You've got gorgeous legs.'

'They're so white.'

'Well, get 'em in the sun then!'

Zed laughed and blushed and stretched them out in front of her. Her legs were all right, apart from the paleness, but they were never going to be like Tamsin's.

'Has he always been that way? Denzil, I mean?'

'Yep. Drove my mum mental. Well, I don't think it was all his fault–'

'And what about you? Did it drive you mental?'

'He used to fight with me, when I lived with them. A lot. An' I didn't like that – and as he got older and stronger, it got more and more scary.'

'I can imagine.'

'So I took up Aikido.'

'Aikido? What's that then?'

'It's a martial art – but one of the best ones for defending yourself while also protecting your attacker from injury. I didn't actually want to hurt him, see.

And it's pretty good for fitness and conditioning and all that jazz. Here, stand up an' I'll demonstrate.'

'It's too hot.'

'Get up on your feet. You have to work for a body like mine.'

Jeez! Not short on confidence then.

Tamsin winked at her and took her hand.

Wait, unless she meant...

'To begin with, you learn about falling safely, and rolling. Shall I show you?'

Zed nodded and Tamsin did a kind of forward somersault over one shoulder and across the grass. She stood up, grinned and said,

'Yeah, it's about joint locks, pins, stuff like that, but Aikido literally means *way of combining forces*. And I like that idea.'

She stepped forward, she was very close now and she gently lifted Zed's wrist. Tamsin's hand was firm, warm and surprisingly soft. Zed had to look at something, anything in the distance.

'I'll show you.'

'Nah – you're all right.' Zed pulled away and stood dazed for a moment before collapsing back down onto the towel and pressing her hands into her eyeballs.

Don't cry. Don't cry. Don't cry.

Tamsin turned away and did that thing where she licked her finger and smoothed down her eyebrows. Then she crouched down, a good arm's length away, but reached across to stroke Zed's hair.

'And did it work?' Zed asked when she could trust her voice again.

'Huh? Oh, well we don't fight anymore, if that's what you mean.' She quickly glanced at Zed before carrying on. 'But he's a lot easier to like these days. He's kinda found what works for him, and all his stories, and funny tics and spending a lot of time by himself – it means that you can actually hang out with him. I don't get so wound up either,' she added after a bit. 'Even when he goes on an' on about those bloody cormorants.'

'Ha–'

'And I've learnt not to expect anything of him, that helps. If he thinks you want something, even if it's something that he might want too, that's when it all goes pear-shaped.'

Okay. Back under control.

'It helps, if you understand a bit, doesn't it?' Zed said.

'Yeah, I guess–'

'I've found out a bit more about what's going on with my sister and I think it might help us – hang out together too.'

'Cool.'

'If she ever comes home, that is.'

'What? She's not here either?'

''Fraid not.'

Tamsin went in to get them both a glass of water and when she came back out, she said, 'Aikido is partly about the physical self-defence stuff, but really it's about mental training – about teaching you to relax in stressful situations. That's the bit that probably helped me the most.'

'I guess we could all do with some of that!' said Zed.

'You should give it a go then. Seriously. My friend Jim took it up when she had really bad eczema an' she reckoned it made all the difference.'

'What about panic attacks?'

'Huh?'

'Would it help with those?'

'Sure. Why not? You'd have to take a look at the root cause, that's what Sensai Kaito would probably say, but it could certainly help with the symptoms.'

Tamsin stared down at her.

'So, do you go the whole hog? The sweaty palms, light head and brain fog thing?'

'Not exactly,' Zed sighed. 'It's more like my throat clamps up and I feel like I've been chucked into a furnace.'

'That's how I feel when I have a really bad crush.'

'Yeah, well, it's excruciating.'

'Tell me about it!'

They locked eyes, for just a moment too long.

'Okay, so I should be–'

'Are you actually going to sit down or what?' said Zed.

Tamsin got out her phone and headphones and they lay back on the towel and took an earpiece each. They lay like that long enough for them to listen to her whole summer playlist for the bike shop.

'Guess I'm not gonna make it to the woods after all,' she said sleepily.

'We could go now if you like?'

'You'd come with me?'

'If you want.'

'Nah, he'd probably rather hang out with those stupid birds anyway.'

'Actually, I'm not sure they *are* that stupid.'

'Oh puleeze, not you as well! Come on,' Tamsin said, getting up and reaching down for Zed's hand. 'Let's go and see Cordelia. I could do with feeding up before I head back.'

When Dad checked in later, he was a mess. The conversation started okay. He asked how Zed was and how her day had been and whether the food had arrived and then his voice cracked.

'What am I doing here, Zed?'

'Earning some money Dad, like you said.'

'How is it that after all the conversations your mum and I had and all the changes we decided to make, how is it that I'm back here again?'

'Have you been to Pisa before then?'

'No! Not here, as in this particular place, but here as in a hotel room, sitting on my own, knackered and knowing I've got a fifteen hour day tomorrow and my family are far away and I don't really know what's going on with them.'

Zed didn't know what to say.

'I've worked so hard to make a new life for us all and nothing has changed.'

'Well–'

'And where the *hell* is your sister?'

Here we go...

'She just needed to see him, Dad.'

'And who is looking after you?'

'Chill out. Cordelia is. I'm fine–'

'Why does she need to see him?'

'She told me everything. All about Luke and the baby. I guess it brought it all up again and she needed someone to–'

'But just when she's getting over it!'

'Well, maybe, I dunno Dad, maybe it's going to take a bit longer, maybe–'

'She needs someone to be there for her. Is that what you were going to say?' He didn't wait for a reply. 'Well, it should have been me!' he growled. Then he burst into tears.

Zed hated it when Dad cried, the funny mewling noises and the deep heaving sobs. It actually made her feel a bit sick.

It got dark and Zed hadn't closed the shutters or turned on any of the lights. She sat staring at the window, nine rectangles of uniform blue-black sky.

She had to try and contact Kerra again.

She needed to find a different way.

Twenty Seven

The following morning Zed made herself go to the boathouse with Cordelia.

They had decided to board up the window, so Zed carried a big piece of plywood and a bag of nails. If she could go there in daylight first, then the thought of going down at dusk – the best time for any kind of paranormal activity according to Amy – might not be quite so sickening. And Cordelia had said in times of strife it was best to keep busy.

At first, Zed had felt uncomfortable about going with her. Was she exposing her to danger? But she reminded herself that Cordelia walked down to the river every morning with Buttons, the path took them right past the smashed window and nothing had happened to her yet.

It was glorious weather, which helped, and Cordelia sang all the way, teaching her Kerra's song, line by line. It felt okay, safe even, singing in the sunshine, with Buttons yapping at their heels. Well, safer than it would do later.

Don't think about it. Not until you have to!

Cordelia said she was keen to take a proper look inside the boathouse, after all these years, but when Zed propped open the door, she seemed reluctant to go inside. She ducked her head under the lintel and peered in, nodding slowly and then stepped back up onto the path and muttered something about letting sleeping dogs lie. A moment later though, she came back to the doorway,

'Well, well, I'd forgotten that bit–'

'What?' said Zed.

'That stove,' said Cordelia, pointing to the corner of the room, 'came from our kitchen. Up at the farm. I think it was an early wedding present from my father. He was very dubious about them actually living down here in the winter and I suppose that was his way of making sure that they stayed warm and dry.'

'Do you think it still works?' Zed asked.

'As long as the chimney's clear. And it looks like it's been cleaned up fairly recently, so I don't see why not.'

Zed held the plywood against the window. The frame was beginning to soften with rot, so it was easy to hammer the nails in through the ply.

When they got back up to the cottage Zed invited herself inside. She said she wanted to run over the words of the song one last time, but she needed something else from Cordelia.

'I was going to ask, if I promise to be really careful, could I borrow your little rag doll?'

'Eh?'

'That one,' said Zed, pointing up to the floppy little cloth doll on the dresser.

'I want to make one of my own for – um, a friend, but – but I don't have a–'

'Pattern?'

'Yeah, yeah – one of those.'

'She's very precious!' Cordelia said after a pause. 'Not much I wouldn't share–'

'I know,' said Zed. 'Please. It will only be for a day or two.'

'Oh, take her then,' Cordelia said sullenly. 'I suppose I've got to be nice in the circumstances. Now bog off while I make my crumble.'

She turned away from Zed and began peeling apples at the sink.

Zed lifted the doll down and let herself out before Cordelia could change her mind.

Twenty Eight

Zed set out as soon as the light began to fade and this time she came prepared. She had a weapon – a hockey stick, and she had body armour too – a bike helmet, Mum's old fencing vest, found in a box in the loft, and a pair of tough gardening gloves that were so rigid with mud that she couldn't bend the fingers. She was also wearing a really stiff leather jacket that Dad had rediscovered in the move and refused to throw away, and Amy's Doc Martens – steel-capped, and two sizes too big. If the cormorants attacked her again, she might not be able to run fast, but at least she'd have some protection from their sharp claws and stabbing beaks. What if they had other plans for her?

Take a breath; hold it; breathe it out slow...

Well, it was best not to think about that!

In her backpack she had matches, newspaper and a couple of dry logs from the bakery. All she needed was kindling to get the stove going and make the boathouse warm and inviting, and so she collected twigs along the path.

She'd also brought a wind-up camping light. Candles were way too creepy and she couldn't risk them blowing out, not when she was alone in the dark.

When the boathouse came into view, she didn't hang around. She'd deliberately left the side door unlocked and with one shove she was in and balancing the lamp on the stern of Dad's rowing boat.

She took out the doll, carefully swathed in bubble wrap. She was so fragile, even the gentlest touch might be enough to damage her. Zed looked around the room for somewhere to put her. She reached for the nearest deckchair, propped up against the wall, but it was a struggle to open. The hinges were rusty and had to be forced, and when she'd put it up, the seat was so rotten that it was obvious that it wouldn't hold a human weight. Fine for a doll though, and Zed laid her carefully in the curve of the fabric, trying to ignore that one button eye.

Zed scrunched up the paper and put it in the stove, piled on the kindling and lit a match. Her hand was shaking. The paper ignited immediately, the flame quickly turning a straight edge into a singed retreating curve, and black dust, but then – whoosh! A hot, orange blaze engulfed the twigs, and filled the corner of the boathouse with a warm, fuzzy glow. She felt herself relaxing, just a bit.

When the flames had died down and the base was white hot, she put in the first of Dad's kiln dried logs and without actually meaning to start, she found herself singing the song Cordelia had taught her. Kerra's song:

> *You penned a song, wrote just for me,*
> *your voice was sweet and strong,*
> *you wrapped your arms around my waist,*
> *and kissed me all day long.*
>
> *Your song I hear it every morn,*
> *it's blowing in the trees,*
> *I hear it as the sun goes down,*
> *it's in the river breeze.*
>
> *Your song will never leave, my love*
> *how e'er the cruel wind moans,*
> *it's in my heart and in my blood,*
> *it's singing in my bones.*

It had sounded quite jolly when Cordelia had sung it, but here in the soft light, no longer struggling to remember the words, Zed found herself really thinking about them for the first time. As she sang of sadness and loss and the need to hold on to something, anything, of a loved one, her voice cracked and caught in her throat.

She did better the second time around, but when she got to the end, she wasn't sure what to do next. Maybe just sit and wait. Maybe–

She felt the temperature drop. Even with all her layers of clothing. She turned and forced herself to look, properly look into the shadows, but there was nothing. No one. She turned back towards the stove, to the soothing undulation of the flames, and there it was.

A face in the mirror.

The face of a young woman standing behind her.

It wasn't a sharp-edged image; there weren't outlines as such, not like the reflection of her own head. It was soft, blurred and watery; the pale brown hair washing into the darkness behind her.

'Sing it again.'

The words were remote and breathy, like an echo on the third or fourth repeat.

'Please–'

Zed started very quietly, trying to smooth out the tremble in her voice.

> *You penned a song, wrote just for me,*
> *your voice was sweet and strong,*
> *you wrapped your arms around my waist,*
> *and kissed me all day long.*

On the last line she heard a faint moan and the image in the mirror rippled, the eyes, nose and ears all tugging against each other. Zed rushed straight into the second verse, knowing that it was this that was drawing the spirit into the room. She held the woman's gaze and sang a little louder, glad she'd gone over the song enough times to be sure of the words and the tune.

There was the voice again a little closer this time, whispering the words, and then singing; harmonising very quietly, but with a richer, warmer tone, a couple of notes above the melody.

They got to the end of the third verse and the young woman held on to the final note, fading it out so slowly that Zed couldn't quite tell when she'd stopped.

She waited.

What next?

Silence, it seemed.

But the image was firming up, as if layer upon layer of paint was being added to a portrait, filling it out. There was the voice again, speaking this time.

'And he was right. It has never left me.'

'Kerra?'

Probably worth checking.

'Why have you called me here, child?'

'I need your help,' said Zed.

'It's hard to rest with a song in your blood, but harder to come back.'

'I'm – sorry about that, but you see, I was wondering–' Zed hadn't exactly thought this bit through.

'Harder to come back and hear our song.'

'I'm sorry,' said Zed again after a pause.

'And hard to feel that feeling again, to feel love.'

'Um–'

'They never found my body. It was the song, you see, weighing down my bones. Down, down, down to the bottom of sea, where I sang to the eels and danced with the gutweed. Singing and dancing, singing and waiting – waiting for him to sing it with me – and I sang and danced and waited until my shoes had turned to mud and my voice silted up, but he never came.'

'He died soon after you.'

'I know that now. I can feel his story, our story here in this room. I can feel his pain.' She flinched. 'He was here all the time, my poor love, caught like a fish in a net.'

'I don't understand,' said Zed.

'He was trapped. By his misery and shame; and death couldn't free him. He's still trapped, somewhere, somewhere near.'

Zed took a deep breath.

'He wasn't the only one trapped.'

Kerra said nothing, but tilted her head and lowered her eyes.

Zed blurted, 'I won't pretend what I'm asking isn't for me. My family, I mean, and maybe some of those who live around us, but it will help him too.'

'Help him how?'

'Free him from – some of that shame. By asking forgiveness for a great betrayal.'

'What betrayal?'

'I need you to speak on his behalf. On our behalf. On behalf of humankind.'

'To whom, child?'

'To the cormorants.'

Kerra waited and then said quietly, 'Eve?'

'Yes.'

Kerra closed her eyes and whispered, 'Ah, now I see it. I see her story too, poor Eve.'

'But it's your story Kerra, because Gawen was grieving for you. It's Eve's story and Gawen's story and your story, but it's also my story, and it's still playing out. I think maybe you can help me to – make a difference – to the ending.'

'And that's why you called me back from the depths of the ocean, to perform this task for you because I'm somehow – to blame?' There was anger in her voice now.

'No! No, I didn't mean– It had to be you because–'

'Well?'

Zed took a moment to get this right.

'I've heard that those who die at sea can return as a cormorant.'

Silence.

'And I think – I believe that it's true.'

Kerra nodded, slowly.

'I once heard something like that, but I'd forgotten–'

'There is still a great deal of bitterness. The cormorants are angry about what happened to Eve and we – my family – have, without meaning to, given them an opportunity to retaliate.'

'I see,' said Kerra. 'And there is no way that you can reach them by yourself?'

'I don't know how to!' said Zed. 'And why should they trust me?'

'But in the shape of a cormorant, I could bridge that gap, between human and bird?'

'Yes, and not only do you know how much Gawen cared for Eve, but also how much he loved you. You know about love, about being in love – and I – I don't.' Zed was on a roll now. 'So you know, better than anyone, that without you he would have been utterly lost and there was no spite towards the bird, just carelessness. A carelessness that cost him his own life as well! And I believe, for all these reasons, you are the only one that can convince them that we should not be enemies, and persuade them to stop seeking revenge.'

'You ask a lot of someone you don't know.'

'I don't know you, but I feel I do – a little. I've heard stories of how kind and caring you were.'

'How? After all this time?'

'Cordelia.'

Zed moved closer to the mirror so she could see the reflection of the doll in the deck chair. Kerra followed her eyes and her face softened,

'Ah, little Corda, my only baban. I'd sing her to sleep every night and tuck up that doll in her cot!'

'She's never forgotten,' said Zed.

'I will do what I can to help you,' said Kerra. She had closed her eyes and her voice was far away again, fragile. 'Love makes you brave, and only the brave can really love. It's so long ago, but I shall try to think of Eve, out on the water.'

'Would this help?' said Zed, reaching into her backpack for the picture Dicky Glynn had given her. She pulled out the sepia photograph of the cormorant and held it up to the mirror.

Kerra spoke again, but there was a rushing, pummelling sound, drowning out her voice. Like water. Waves? No, more like a beating – and the pale face was fading, the image pulsing, but getting weaker and weaker.

'When I have news, I'll send you a sign.'

'Tell them I'm a believer.'

The mirror went black, for a moment. Then the black retreated and there were wings, feathers, that serpentine neck twisting up, a beak and an emerald eye.

Twenty Nine

Zed went to visit Mum at the hospital. It was over thirty miles away and she took the bus. Well, two buses and a long walk at either end. According to the council website, the whole journey should have taken an hour and fifty three minutes. Let's just say that was optimistic.

Mum was on the fourth floor and the corridor that led to her ward had mint green walls. There were picture hooks and little laminated signs, but no pictures.

She was in the first bay by the door and looked so pale, flat and reliant on the pillows propping her up, it was as if a photo had been stitched onto them.

'I can't sleep,' she whispered. 'That woman over there was moaning all through the night. She's proper confused. No idea where she is.'

'How's your arm?' asked Zed.

'First lot of antibiotics didn't do anything, so they're trying something else. Painkillers are good though.'

'Have you spoken to Dad?'

'Yes.'

'And?'

Mum sighed. 'And what?'

'Does he seem okay to you?'

'I've got nothing spare to – worry about your dad. We'll keep talking. That's all I can say.'

'Have you talked to Amy?'

'Yes. She rang to tell me where she was, and why. I told her I understood.'

'What if she doesn't come back?'

'Oh love, I can't think about that either.'

Zed crossed her arms and then her legs and then she tucked her foot behind her calf. She wedged her knotted body into the back of the padded chair and stared out of the window.

'Maybe we were wrong to bring her down here,' said Mum after a bit. 'If she really hates it – I mean, who are we to tell her what to do?'

'But–'

'I told her to be sensible.'

'What do you mean by *sensible?*' asked Zed. She wanted to know if she could tell, now that she knew, that Mum was keeping something from her. That she was protecting Amy's secret.

'I meant that I trusted her – to work out what she needs to – to make peace with the situation and – and–' She pointed to a beaker of water with a straw, which Zed passed to her. She took a sip and tried again. 'I said I trusted she'd make sure she protects herself from–'

'From what?' Zed interrupted. She knew she sounded sulky, but she couldn't help it.

Mum closed her eyes. 'I was going to say unnecessary hurt, but I know she's told you, so yes, from *that* too.'

'Why didn't you tell me?'

'She didn't want me to.'

'So?'

'She was in such a different place from you.'

'What? Do you mean that I don't have a boyfriend?'

'No! Well, yes, maybe. You just seemed a long way from even being interested in that kind of thing. You had your friends; you were doing well at school and it didn't seem necessary to involve you in – all that heartache.'

'Heartache doesn't have to come in the form of boys you know.'

'I know that Zed.'

'And if you lock me out of those conversations, *Zed is fine, Zed wouldn't understand, Zed will be fine*, then you never give me a chance to share my feelings – *my* heartache. It's always about you or Dad or Amy. Not because I'm the youngest, but because everyone just assumes I'm alright.'

'*Are* you alright?'

'No,' said Zed. 'But you've already told me you've got nothing spare. You're in hospital – again. And in pain – again! So I guess now isn't the time.'

'I'm sorry.'

'And I hate hospitals,' said Zed. 'Especially since last time–'

Mum nodded. 'I'm sorry,' she said again. 'I'm sorry for all the heartache *I've* caused you. I'm not sure I've ever actually said that.'

'That's not what I meant.'

'Maybe not, but I regret it hugely. Putting you through it.'

Zed couldn't say it was okay because it wasn't. It really wasn't.

'Look, I know I wasn't exactly thinking straight, but you weren't meant to be the one to find me,' Mum added.

Oh hell. Zed could feel the tears coming. If she started now, it would be a full on sobbing snot storm.

'And whatever happens to us, as a family, I promise I'll never allow myself to get that low like – to feel that desperate–' Mum took another sip of water. 'To do something like that again.'

Zed looked at her feet, then her hands, then her watch and tried not to blink.

'Is Cordelia looking after you? She left a very sweet message saying that she would.'

'I've never eaten so many eggs!'

While waiting at the bus stop, Zed messaged Tamsin with a link to a *Cat v. Dog* Aikido film. She called back straight away, her face entirely filling the screen.

'Ha – they've even got the right kit on,' she said, swinging her phone around and getting out of the way so that Zed could see the white jacket and black trousers hanging on the back of her bedroom door. The dog was a black and white Collie and the cat had white fur and black paws.

'What's that?' asked Zed. 'Go back.'

Tamsin panned round.

'Stop. Right there.'

The camera wobbled and then settled on a large wooden cage.

'Have you got a guinea pig or what?'

'Ah, it's about time you met Big Mac!' said Tamsin and the screen went all wonky and all Zed could hear was, 'Come on, come and meet my new friend,' and then Tamsin appeared again holding a ball of prickles with pale pink paws, a white tummy and a little brown nose that reminded Zed of the leather buttons Nanny Pam had on her favourite camel coat.

'What on earth is that?' said Zed.

'An African pygmy hedgehog.' Tamsin picked up one of its tiny paws and waved it at the camera.

'It looks like one of those coconut macaroons.'

'That's why it's called Big Mac.'

'The *big* being ironic, obviously!'

'You got it. My dad bought her for me. He said she reminded him of me because she's very short-sighted an' if she's feeling defensive she rolls up into a spiky ball.'

'Are you short-sighted?'

'Yup. Very. I wear contact lenses.'

'Oh cool,' said Zed. 'I've always wanted to wear those ones that give you different coloured eyes. Quite fancy green.'

'Well, why don't you?'

'Dunno really. People might laugh?'

'No one down here knows what colour your eyes are though, do they? Except me and I won't tell.'

'Well–'

'You're starting afresh. It's a blank page and you can be exactly who you wanna be! That's actually pretty exciting.'

'I hadn't really thought of it like that,' said Zed.

'Well, I would if I were you,' said Tamsin. 'But I'm not saying you *should* change the colour of your eyes. They seem pretty perfect to me, the way they are.'

The bus arrived. Zed got on, dug out her return ticket and lurched to the seats along the back row before lifting up the phone again and carrying on their conversation.

'Show me round your bedroom, then.'

The floor was a mess of dumped clothes, mugs and wet towels. The duvet was twisted into a knot at the bottom of the bed and a crumpled pillow was propped at an angle against the headboard. A graphic novel, bent back at the spine, had been discarded, face down on the sheet, alongside a pile of magazines.

'It's not the tidiest,' said Tamsin, doing a quick grimace into the camera.

'Go to the notice board.'

Tamsin zoomed in on the wall above the hedgehog cage. It was covered in cards, photos and posters and – a certificate.

'What's that for?' said Zed.

'Um – I need to have a bit of a clear out, actually.' The camera moved sharply to the left.

'Not so fast. What's it for?' said Zed again. 'Tell me.'

'Promise you won't tease me?'

'I promise.'

'Getting ten out of ten for my seven times table!'

Lucky it wasn't a pinky promise! Zed burst out laughing. She laughed so loudly that the bus driver jerked his head up to the mirror to see what was going on.

'Are you for real?'

Tamsin appeared back in the screen, trying very hard to look cross.

'Alright, I know–' she said, giving up. 'But it's from primary school an' I loved that teacher.'

'Really?'

'Yeah, really! For quite a few years she was the love of my life, no kidding. Now back off otherwise I'll go all spiky and roll into a ball!'

There were posters of cyclists in mountains and deserts, and the *Birds in the Bladderwrack* girls all waving rainbow flags on a march in Plymouth. There was a one of a really angry Tamsin shoving a flyer in someone's face.

'What's that all about?' said Zed.

'We were petitioning shoppers at the supermarket in Tremarrak to strip off all their plastic packaging an' leave it at the till. I got a bit feisty.'

'So I see!'

There was a series of pictures of her wearing fluorescent yellow knee pads and doing tricks on a skateboard.

'You're a skater too, eh? A girl of many talents!' said Zed.

'What's yours, then?'

'Huh?'

'What's your hidden talent?'

'Not sure I've got one.'

'I bet you have.'

'Don't think I do actually,' said Zed. 'I guess I'm just too busy being scared.'

Thirty

When she finally got back to the house it was getting dark. She marched around closing all the shutters, turning on all the lights and then went up to Amy's room to get her speakers and brought them down to the kitchen. That way she could play her music loudly enough to pretend that she wasn't spending another night by herself, in a knackered, eerie old house, just up the lane from a wood filled with–

Enough!

She got a glass of juice from the fridge and sat down at the kitchen table with her origami book when there was a tap at the back door.

Zed froze. Cordelia never knocked, just pushed open the door and announced herself. Who else would come around at this time of night? In the dark?

Zed looked around frantically.

A frying pan maybe? Or a wooden rolling pin?

Another knock–

Okay– Okay–

She picked up the phone, tapped 999 and held her finger over *send*.

'Who is it?' she called out.

'It's your supper! Now open the door!'

Tamsin had cycled all the way from Clewmor over to Tremarrak to get fish and chips and then back to Tremelin. She barged into the kitchen, took off her helmet and plonked two parcels on the table. The fat and vinegar had soaked through the paper leaving dark glossy patches. The smell was divine.

'Wasn't my idea!' she admitted. 'Cordelia said you shouldn't be on your own an' if I didn't come up, she'd have to come over and she's rather partial to her own bed!'

Zed was smiling so much her cheeks began to throb.

'I was on my own last night,' she said.

'Yeah, but rent-a-granny thought Amy was here. It's taken her a day or two to work out why it's so quiet!'

Tamsin put the fish and chips in the oven to warm up a bit and Zed went upstairs to drag Amy's mattress into her room. She looked around for clean bedding, but had no idea where Mum had put it. At least when she'd been in hospital last time, they'd been in the house long enough to know where everything lived, and Granny Steph had moved in to make sure they ate proper meals, got to school on time and always hung up their towels after a shower! Zed threw her dirty knickers into the laundry basket and made her bed, although having seen the state of Tamsin's bedroom she wasn't sure why she was bothering, and she changed her t-shirt. Then she washed her face, cleaned her teeth and put on a smidgen of Amy's mascara.

'So, do you really not know where *your* mum is?' she asked Tamsin as she came down the stairs.

'Up in Bristol last time we heard. I get a text once in a while and she writes to Cordelia. Denzil too, but she'll send them to one of his mates so it's sometimes a while before he gets them. It would help if he'd get a mobile, but he won't, of course, especially now that I've suggested it more than once.'

'That's tough,' said Zed.

'Yeah, well. She sends me some cash occasionally too. I bet I earn more than she does, but I guess it makes her feel better!'

They took their food into the sitting room and sat side by side on the floor with their backs to the sofa. Zed picked up the TV remote control and put it by her side. Just in case the conversation lagged.

'Your dad seems really cool, though.'

'He is. I can talk to him about anything. I've had a few awkward conversations with him over the last year or so, you know, working out who I am kinda stuff and he's cool with everything. Just wants me to be happy.'

'And are you?'

'Wow! Straight to the core, eh Zed!'

'Sorry – it's just–'

'Nah, you're okay. I like it.'

She leaned into Zed so that their thighs were touching, and when she pulled back Zed let her leg go loose at the hip joint so that it stayed with Tamsin's and fell away to the side. That moment, skin on skin – it was like brushing velvet.

'I wish I could talk to my mum a bit more and that she like, had a phone number that stayed the same for more than a few weeks. An' I really wish she'd come and visit us. She says she will, and soon, but it hasn't happened yet. I rushed up here that day I first met you because Cordelia said she was gonna

140

call her and I wanted to be there, but she never did, and that really got to me.'

Zed's hand drifted towards Tamsin's and then it just seemed to stop and hover in mid-air. She quickly pulled it back.

'It's why I was so grouchy. I didn't hear your sister screaming, even though Cordelia told me about it later, just saw a mum, a dad and their two kids all excited to be moving into their big new home, all together under one roof.'

'You were pretty grouchy.'

'Yeah, well, um – sorry about that.'

She turned to Zed and gave her a sheepish little smile. 'So, am I happy? Well, I guess what would make me really happy is to have someone special, just for me.'

Oh flippin', freakin' hell—

Zed couldn't take her eyes off her toes.

'I've got friends, really good friends, and I thought that might be enough, for the time being at least. An' there's my brother, he's the only boy I've ever really cared for, apart from Dad of course, but then, well, you know–'

Zed nodded, her fingers curling around the remote control.

'But I've realised – that I want something more than that.'

Deep breaths Zed.

They sat in silence for a moment. It was a very weird kind of silence.

'I'm stressing you out a bit here, aren't I? I can tell–'

'Shall we just–'

'Yeah, let's eat–'

Tamsin got up first thing to go to work, which couldn't have been easy as they'd watched films – some silly comedy and then a slap-stick heist – until about three in the morning. The thought of saying goodbye made Zed feel so inexplicably sad that she pretended to be asleep as her friend crept around the room gathering up her stuff. She then waited until she was sure Tamsin had left Tremelin – and hadn't just gone over to Cordelia's for breakfast – before coming downstairs, opening the shutters and putting on the kettle.

Zed spent the morning alternating between drifting around the house and then drifting around the garden. She didn't want to go into Clewmor, but she couldn't settle down to anything at home. She kept telling herself she'd done everything she could and she just had to wait, but it was hard. Waiting and hoping. Hoping for a sign.

She flipped through a pile of books, started watching another film, one that Caitlin said was the funniest thing ever, but gave up after ten minutes and stomped up the stairs and along the landing, picking at the peeling paper and rubbing the stains on the floorboards with her big toe, then she wandered back down again counting the missing spindles.

She wandered out into the garden and dragged her feet through the long grass. She went up to the outbuildings to have a look at the lawn mowers. One was electric, but she couldn't see an extension lead, and the other was an old rotary one, almost entirely rusted up.

She thought about calling someone. Caitlin maybe. To tell her the film was dire. It would be lovely to hear her voice, just to hear any young, chatty, familiar voice, but did she really want to hear all about everyone's epic summer holidays? What they got up to at Keisha's party, how much they earned waitressing for Jake's mum and the day trip to Brighton they'd all been planning the week before she left?

And how would she explain what was going on down here, where would she begin? And if she was honest and said that things weren't working out so well, was there a chance that they'd go back? Caitlin would ask her. She knew she would, and she really couldn't go there.

She sat down on the back doorstep and started flicking through everyone's posts. Pictures were easier than words. If she scrolled though fast enough then most of them didn't even seem like real people – just pretend people, the people they were all pretending to be, and she wasn't that interested, not really, she was just swiping her screen, passing the time.

What the –?

She stopped and scrolled back. To Beth sitting on Kabir's lap.

Zed felt dizzy – more than dizzy, properly sick. She tried to turn her phone off and burst into tears.

She looked again. It was still there. Bethany with her arm around Kab's shoulders and her face buried in his neck. That wasn't the way friends were with each other. That was – and it shouldn't matter. It didn't matter – except – except– She threw down her phone, wrapped her arms around her middle and rocked herself back and forth. It shouldn't matter. It didn't matter. It shouldn't matter – but it did.

Thirty One

Cordelia and Buttons kept popping across to check on Zed. In fact, Buttons seemed to be spending more time in Zed's garden than Cordelia's. It was probably to do with the improved odds of getting a stick thrown, but it felt like more than that. It felt as if he was looking out for her.

Animal intuition.

And she knew all about that now, didn't she?

It was no surprise then, to hear him yapping under her bedroom window. Again.

She was lying on her bed staring at her ceiling, her phone resting on her chest. By cross referencing the posts of everyone in her class (her old class!) – some of them were very snap happy – she'd worked out when Kabir and Beth had got together and pretty much what they'd been doing since. Not everything they'd been doing, that would be like, really wrong, obviously, but they seemed to be hanging out together – a lot! And Beth looked so happy, in every single photo. It wasn't some fake attempt to make her friends jealous – look at me loving my great life – that thing some people did to make others feel like losers, it wasn't all choreographed selfies and smiley emojis, this looked like the real deal.

Zed's stomach flipped over and then twisted itself into a little tight knot.

The blushing, the touching, the eye contact – did that mean she had imagined it?

Buttons was properly yapping. She put her phone down and leaned out of the window. As soon as he saw her, he leaped up and down in a frenzy of excitement.

'Okay, okay!' she shouted down.

It didn't matter did it? The point, Zed knew, was how *she* had felt.

She went downstairs and Buttons hurtled around to meet her at the back door. She looked around for a stick, but when she threw one, he didn't chase after it as usual, he continued to dance around at her feet instead. Zed, who wasn't going to go chasing off into the undergrowth unnecessarily, looked around for another stick, but Buttons was so frantic to stay close to her that she kept nearly tripping over him.

'What's up, pup?' she asked. He bounced away and waited. Nothing happened so he came back, sat on her foot for just a moment, nuzzled her knee and then sprang up and away again. She looked at him.

'What?' she asked again. 'What do you want?'

This time he ran out onto the lawn and she followed. He bounded back towards her with his pink tongue lolling out, panting with all the exertion. She took a few steps forward and he ran around her several times, before running off towards the stream. He was heading for the largest of the two weeping willows and when Zed got close he dived into the trailing green leaves, just like she'd done the day after they moved in. When she didn't follow immediately, his head poked through and he barked at her. His meaning was pretty clear. She pushed the branches aside and stepped into the green space within.

And then she saw it. At the bottom of the trunk, nestled into the muddy joint between two roots, was an egg. It was a pale, chalky blue egg. Just the one. There was no sign of a nest and no sign of a bird, but she knew what it was. Denzil's painting had captured the colour perfectly. It was a cormorant egg. It was a sign. The sign she'd been waiting for.

Thirty Two

Zed didn't wait until dusk this time. She ran back to the house, put on her improvised armour, which she'd dumped in a pile in the corner of the boot room, grabbed her hockey stick and set off for the boathouse. Just as she was rushing out of the door, she snatched Cordelia's doll from the shelf above the lintel.

It was a warm day and very quickly Zed felt hot and rather silly wearing a fencing vest, oversized leather jacket and boots, bike helmet and gardening gloves. The hockey stick and doll didn't help either, but there was no way she was going into the woods without protection. She might be a bit troubled, but she didn't have a death wish.

Some walkers had stopped to look at their map on the corner by the low cottage and when they glanced up to greet her, they couldn't help smirking. One of them said, 'You look like you're having fun!'

She ignored him and clomped past.

The other one said, 'You're dressed for a snowstorm!' He looked up at the sky and waved his stick. 'Do you know something we don't?' he called after her.

'You have no idea, turd brain!' said Zed under her breath.

When she got to the boathouse, the door was ajar. She stopped, statue still, and listened.

She took a couple of steps closer and attempted to peer through one of the un-boarded windows. The layers of leaves above diffused the sunshine, but the softer light still bounced off the glass, making it impossible to see inside. She'd forgotten about her helmet and as she leaned in, it clunked against the window frame. She sprang back and waited. Silence.

Zed crept along to the door, nudged it back with her hockey stick, as far as it would go, and pressed herself flat against the wall outside. Again – nothing. So, after a moment or two, she took a deep breath and told herself she had to go in.

Was this what Kerra meant? Zed couldn't think of anywhere else that she might be expected to go.

Was it a trap? She took another deep breath and stuffed that thought away again, or at least under a pile of other thoughts, the most pressing of which was, what should she actually do? She propped the doll in the chair, like before, and stood in front of the mirror. Maybe she could adopt the same approach as the other night; a warm stove, soft light and the familiar song. She was about to start singing when – she didn't hear anything or see anything, just felt it – like the space had shrunk a little, that she was sharing it. And then voice, louder and more throaty than last time, filled the boathouse.

'I've done as you asked, child.'

Zed looked about, but there was nothing to see. Neither in the mirror nor the room.

'Where – where are you?' she asked.

'I'm here,' said the voice, 'as you wished, and I've been there, as you wished, to see my cormorant brothers and sisters. They welcomed me and we gathered at the bend in the river. We swam and hung our wings out to dry. We feasted and while we digested, I told them a tale of a man and a woman and a bird.'

'Did they listen?'

'It was a tragic tale, but one without a villain.'

'And–?'

'Except possibly the sea, but they know her and her wily ways.'

'And did you make them understand? Will they stop this – this hostility?' asked Zed urgently.

'It's not the first time man has conspired against the cormorant,' she rasped, 'Gawen's was not the first crime.'

'But man has always hunted animals,' said Zed. 'Just as animals hunt animals. It is the natural order of things and our prey don't all set out to destroy us!'

'Killing to eat is one thing. Killing to prevent others from eating into your profits is another.'

Zed couldn't argue with that.

'And maybe those other creatures that you talk of don't have the wherewithal,' the voice continued with a harsh cough, 'the intelligence, the wisdom and the skills–'

'Will they forgive us?'

'I've done your bidding, child. A truce has been called. Securing it though, is up to you.'

'What do I need to do?'

'Humans and cormorants will gather on the sandbanks. Tomorrow, at the end of the day.'

'Tomorrow?' said Zed. 'Humans? How many?'

'It's not about numbers, child, but the strength of your intention. The cormorants have some friends among you, they know that, but they want brave new allies with whom they can further an understanding. If you wish to share the land and water, they want proof of tolerance and esteem. They want to know you can live in peace.'

'I think – I can only – there might only be two of us,' said Zed.

'Then you must speak, in advance, on behalf of more.'

'I can do that,' Zed replied.

'And you must show willing by celebrating their presence and guiding us all though a ceremony. I've told them our story, but you must share with them your truth.'

'I can do that!' said Zed again.

'The curse began with cormorant blood. It should end with a shared blessing.'

Zed nodded.

'And then you must go away and spread respect and good words like they spread their wings.'

'We will honour the cormorants, I promise,' said Zed. 'Both tomorrow and afterwards.'

'Then two will be enough.'

Thirty Three

Even two was going to be a challenge. Zed tried to call Amy. She lost track of how many times she'd tried calling her, but it kept going onto voicemail.

'Pick up!' she found herself yelling into the phone. 'Please call me. It's an emergency,' but either Amy was constantly on the phone to someone else, or she'd let her battery go flat, which was much more likely. Other more disturbing explanations began to form themselves. Zed knew Amy had spoken to Mum, but that was a couple of days ago and she'd heard nothing since.

And twenty-four hours! That was all she had. Twenty-four hours to pull together some kind of ritual to convince the cormorants that she and Amy, representing the whole of mankind, regretted all the cruelty of the past and were committed to a new relationship based on acceptance, respect and friendship.

No challenge there then!

Only twenty-four hours to pull herself together too. The thought of walking out onto an exposed stretch of sand with no cover and no means of defending herself, knowing the birds were coming, the thought of being surrounded by them, squawking and swooping towards her with their claws spread, ready to rip into her flesh, those pincer-sharp beaks, those cruel eyes.

Not now– Please, not now–

She felt the familiar sensation; the crushing in her chest and the pain as her ribs tried to resist. She put her hand in front of her nose to try to prove to herself that air was actually still going into her lungs, but everything in the room started pulsing, in and out of focus. It was going black around the edges. She couldn't do it – she couldn't do it–

Get a grip. Get a grip. Get a grip.

She couldn't do it alone. That was for sure.

Where the hell was Amy? If she called back tomorrow, it would be too late. Tonight was too late! She needed to get on that coach now. Be on it right now.

Zed looked at her phone again and found herself scrolling down to *L*.

Really?

Anything was worth a try.

'What's up, Zee?' He'd always called her that. It was really annoying.

'Um, yes, it's me.'

'I know. Your name comes up when you call.'

He spoke quietly and with pauses so long that she wondered if her signal was dodgy again.

'Um, hi Luke. I was wondering if you're with – if, um – Actually, I was wondering how you – how you are?'

Jeez! Where did that come from?

There was another long pause.

'I'm doing good, considering–'

'Cool.'

'And you?'

'Yeah, um, fine.'

'So look, I'm at work–'

Work? Luke is at work?

'Wow! That sounds good.'

'If you say so.'

'What are you doing?'

'Oh, just stuff in a warehouse, packing up boxes, you know.'

Zed didn't really. Not that it mattered.

'So I can't really chew the fat.' he said.

'Is Amy with you?'

'She left a couple of hours ago. I put her on the coach.'

'Oh, I see,' said Zed. 'So, so she's on her way home? Now?'

'Yeah – that's what I just said.'

'Right.'

'She wanted to get back, you know, and sort herself out for next year. She was so excited and she deserves to be, doesn't she? She did good.'

It took Zed a moment – *of course, her exam results!*

'I gave her some money for a cab at your end. I know your mum's not well and your dad's up here, with your gran, isn't he, just got back from his conference in Italy. He is super stressed. Sounds like they worked him pretty hard and he has to some big presentation tomorrow, apparently.'

'Yes – wait, how do you know that?'

'I took her round to see him.'

'You went to see my dad?' Zed asked, incredulous.

'Well, no. I dropped her there. I had a shift and, you know, there didn't seem a great deal of point–'

'No, I guess not,' said Zed.

'I mean, the idea was to cheer him up!' And Zed and Luke almost had a laugh together.

'Look, I've got to go,' he said.

'Sure.'

'It was cool that she came up, even if only for a couple of days. She went into school for her results, and we got to talk through some stuff, a lot of stuff I guess and – and in the end I figured it was cool to see her getting on with things. I'm pleased for her, you know?'

'Yeah, I know,' said Zed.

Amy got back at midnight. She'd been researching sixth form colleges on the coach and she was so excited that she was up for anything. Which was good because they had a lot of work to do and Zed was pretty worked up. She had promised a lot, a hell of a lot, and thoughts of how to deliver were beginning to freak her out, but at least it kept her focused on her part of the deal, and that was surely better than thinking about what the birds might want to do, if she got it wrong!

Okay, so, a ceremony...

And one that worked without words. Unless Kerra could translate? But they couldn't rely on that, Kerra might think her job was done and not turn up. Anyway, there had to be better ways to commemorate their new understanding, and it wasn't as if she couldn't use words at all, she would need them to get her meaning straight in her own head and they might be useful to keep Amy in the picture. That was if she really could depend on her help.

"Course, you can!' said Amy. 'I've told you, haven't I? I just need to make a few more calls and then I'm all yours. Whatever it is you want to play out, I'm playing–'

'It's not a game, Amy.'

'Yeah, no, sure, I get that.'

'You know how scared I am of those birds.'

'Look, I'm all over it, okay?'

Zed spent most of the night on the internet looking for inspiration. The following morning, she'd come up with a plan of sorts, and bleary-eyed, she cycled into Clewmor leaving Amy at home with instructions to turn the Kilner jar of yeast starter into some kind of decorative chalice.

'How the hell am I supposed to do that?' asked Amy.

'You got a GCSE in Art now, remember?' said Zed. 'You'll think of something.'

Amy grunted. 'And remind me what we're doing here?'

'It's going to be another *blót* if you like. To reverse the curse.'

'Right. With a load of birds. Tonight. Down on the river.'

'Yep,' said Zed.

'And Kerra told you to do this? In the boathouse?'

'Yes,' said Zed. 'I tried again without all the tricksy stuff. I just sang to her and she came.'

'Keeping it real, sis!' said Amy, punching Zed on the arm.

'You've got to promise to embrace it. Seriously. If we get it right, it will change our lives, Ames. I mean, where they're going–'

'Mine's already changing.'

'Well–'

'But, lucky for you I don't have any friends to go celebrating with!'

'It will be a kind of celebration.'

'Mmm – not really what I meant.'

When Zed got back from her shopping trip, she went up to her room and spent the afternoon doing origami. It started off as a way of calming herself down, a bit of an interlude before getting down to business, but then she had an idea. There wasn't a cormorant in the book Amy gave her, the closest she could get was a pelican, but she had a look online and was amazed to find instructions and even a tutorial given by a Japanese girl, who couldn't have been more than seven or eight. Zed had a couple of dummy runs, working and re-working the folds to get them just right, and then she made nineteen cormorants, one for every year of Kerra's life. She threaded them onto a long piece of cotton and packed them in the top of her rucksack.

She looked at the clothing she'd worn on her last two trips to the boathouse. She looked at her hockey stick and for a moment she thought it might be sensible to– No, it was about trust!

Amy, with her skinny black jeans, black jacket and ink black hair, looked as close to cormorant as it was possible for a human being to get. Zed riffled through her drawers to see if she could find something similar and came up with black leggings and an old black sweatshirt that she'd used for a school production of *Cats*. If she wore black too, maybe that would put the birds at ease.

Shame there were no green contact lenses knocking about!

And then she had an even better idea. On her desk were two half-finished papier mâché masks. The basic head shapes were done, each one dried out and stiff, but they hadn't been painted. She went down to the kitchen, where Amy was putting the finishing touches to the Kilner jar. She had covered the glass in layers of tissue paper, stuck on beads, sequins and bits of lace and she was shaking a pot of glitter over the lid.

'Nearly done,' she said.

'It looks great, Amy.'

'Yeah, I'm pretty pleased with it.'

'But, I'm afraid that was just the warmup–'

'What? Don't push your luck!'

'Come on. Get to it,' said Zed, ignoring her protests. 'And we'll need black paint, more sequins and cardboard.'

Thirty Four

They set off in the early evening, under a bright blue sky. The sun was behind them and wispy trails of white cloud hovered high above the trees. Zed was carrying her rucksack and Amy carried a large cardboard box. Neither of the girls spoke to start with, but in the silence, the *what ifs* went round and around Zed's brain. She had to bite her tongue not to share them with her sister, especially as her biggest fear was, what if Amy changed her mind and decided to go home?

So, she filled the silence with other words, any words–

'So, what are you going to do for your A levels?'

'Haven't decided. Maybe Photography?'

'When do you think Dad will be coming back?'

'He said the day after tomorrow.'

'D'you reckon Clewmor Hall will reopen soon?'

'Do we care?'

'I wonder what happened to the science teacher on the roof?'

'Dunno.'

'Or the guy who drives the ferry?'

'Look will you just–'

'It was actually quite nice to talk to Luke!'

'Yeah?' said Amy.

'Yeah. Was it okay? Seeing him, I mean?'

Amy thought for a moment.

'He knows I'm not going back, to live, I mean, and he's sad, of course, but not in a moody way. Not anymore. He's sad – but in a slightly, kind of, more upbeat way. Does that make sense?'

'Um – I think so,' said Zed.

'It seems the whole nearly-being-a-Dad thing has actually made him want to get himself together. Made him realise, when he does do it, he's got to do it right.'

'That makes sense.'

'And with someone who really wants it too.'

'Good for him!'

Amy looked at her.

'I really mean it!'

'And he said he was proud. He actually said that. Even though I wasn't his to be proud of anymore.' Amy's eyes filled with tears, but she quickly blinked them away.

'Well, that's nice of him.'

'Yeah. It is.'

It was low tide and once they'd passed under the viaduct, the stream to the left was little more than a dribble of water, washing over the stones and silt that clogged up the middle of the muddy basin. As the boathouse came into view, so did the reeds that ran alongside the main river, blocking even a glimpse of the water when it was so low in the channel. Amy slowed down when they got close to the first window, stepping away from the path to peer in.

'Was that the mirror?' she said, pointing over to above the stove. 'That little one there?'

'Yes,' said Zed.

'Nice.'

The path led round to the right and, as before, it took Zed a while to find a route through the nettles and brambles, out onto the marshy bank. They removed their shoes and left them propped up against the trunk of a large beech tree. The low tide didn't mean there was any less squelch as they picked their way across the grass – with each step the water filled their footprints – but when they reached the river itself, there were islands of ribbed, sandy sediment and that provided firmer footing.

'This is the place,' said Zed, looking around and choosing the broadest bank of sand. It was flat and unlike some of the others upstream, that sparkled in the sunshine, it was the colour of dull sludge. It was close to the trees though.

Keep busy. Keep focused!

She opened her rucksack, carefully lifted out her origami birds and started hanging them in the branches, but her hands were shaking and she couldn't tie the knots. Amy watched her for a moment then took over, saying, 'You know, assuming Kerra was right and the cormorants have called a truce–'

'Yes?' said Zed weakly.

'Then I think this is really going to help. Help you get to grips with your panic attacks or phobia or whatever it is. I mean it's like the ultimate exposure therapy!'

154

'If you say so,' said Zed.

'Seriously. Not only are you going to spend some time hanging out with birds, but if it's a good experience, if you pull it off, I mean, then that memory will replace the bad ones.'

'If *we* pull it off,' said Zed.

'Yeah, *we*, whatevs—'

Amy built a fire. She was surprisingly good at it and before long they were able to cook two of the pieces of mackerel that Zed had bought that morning. Even though she was far too nervous to actually be hungry, they smelled good and Zed felt her dry mouth fill with saliva. They were not to be eaten yet however, and Amy left them wrapped in foil on the sand.

Zed reached into the front pocket of her rucksack and pulled out the jar of yeast starter. They dug a little hole in the wet sand and wedged it in. Then she pulled out the blue tourmaline crystal she'd bought for Kerra and a new stone that she'd got from Clewmor Crystals that morning.

'What's that one for, then?' said Amy. Zed pulled out her phone and scrolled to the photo she'd taken in the shop.

> *Malachite – a good balancing stone to help to feel stable, safe*
> *and secure in opening your heart to all types of love.*

'Seemed kind of appropriate,' said Zed.

They opened up the cardboard box and lifted out two beautiful black shiny masks, the paint only just dry. They'd cut away around the mouth and built up the front with layers of damp paper which they'd draped over cut-up egg boxes and dried with Amy's hair dryer. Then they'd stuck on narrow paper beaks, each one made around a frame of pipe cleaners. Zed had cut out holes for them to see through, and surrounded them with circles of green sequins. Just below they had dabbed on streaks of buttercup yellow.

They took a moment to admire their work, then they looked at each other and nodding with approval, they carefully placed the masks on top of their heads, before pulling them down to cover their faces and tying up the ribbons at the back. It wasn't meant to be a transformation, not like Kerra's, but a gesture of alliance. If it offered any protection or even made the birds think twice about attacking one of their own, that was a bonus, right?

And so the two cormorant girls sat on the sandbanks, facing the woods, to wait. Amy reached into her bag and pulled out a roll-up.

'You can't do that! Not now!' hissed Zed.

'Hey,' said Amy, lighting up, 'smoking weed is a spiritual act, it cleans the body and mind and it heals the soul.'

'That's just bollocks, and you know it!'

'It's a little parting gift from Luke. Now seems as good a time as any; and then, I'm done. Turning over a new leaf. All squeaky clean.'

Amy offered Zed a drag, but she refused. The smell was bad enough.

'Did you know Beth and Kabir are an item?'

'Ouch.'

'Not you as well!'

'Whaddya mean?'

'Mum wanted me and Kab to get it together.'

Amy turned to look at Zed, her beak knocking the side of her sister's mask. 'Well, that was never going to happen, was it?'

Zed shook her head.

'But Beth – well, I get it.'

'Do you?' said Zed.

'Sure. She's hot. I fancy her myself.'

The sky was changing colour, first threads of pale yellow light streaking across the blue above the treetops and then the thin clouds turning into grey smudges against the pink and orange sky. As the fire died down Zed was glad of her sweatshirt and she pulled the frayed cuffs over her hands. She looked over to her paper birds, gently swaying in the breeze and up to the leaves above, where a loose knot of twigs balanced in the fork of the branch. Was that a cormorant's nest? As if in answer to her question, she heard a long drawn out *caaaaw*. Zed jerked around and grabbed Amy's hand.

'Where is it?'

Amy looked into the undergrowth. The light was fading though, and it was hard to see – but then, a rustle in the grass and the first cormorant stepped boldly onto the sand. The girls stayed completely still.

Breathe... Breathe slowly; ride it out.

It spread, then closed its wings, as if shaking out an umbrella. It straightened its neck, dipped its beak and jolted its head to one side. That green stud of an eye, a surveillance camera, checking them out.

'You were right, it is just like a crochet hook,' whispered Amy, hardly moving her mouth.

'What?' said Zed.

'That beak. It's–'

'Sshh...'

They felt a rush in the air behind them and swung around to see three cormorants, their webbed feet splayed out before them, coming in to land on the sand bank and folding their glossy black wings into their bodies as they

156

tipped themselves upright. Another four were descending in a long slow glide, braking into the shallow water before stepping out and shaking themselves dry. Zed turned back to see two more coming out from behind the clumps of reeds under the trees, and another two, flying down from the left. She shut her eyes, just for a moment, and everything shrank into a black hole. She couldn't feel her body – or her fear. Nothing. It was like watching herself through a lens, which was weird, but okay. Especially if it meant she stayed calm.

Whether it was the embers of the fire or the girls themselves that the birds were unsure of, they kept their distance, taking positions around the edge of the little island.

Amy glanced at Zed. She was waiting for her to do something. This was totally her call.

One of the cormorants moved towards them. Amy, who was still holding onto Zed's hand, clutched it a little tighter. The bird stopped several feet away and dipped its head, as if awaiting instructions.

Very slowly Zed got to her feet, dragging Amy up with her. She lowered her head, halfway between a nod and a bow, and said 'Welcome', just loud enough to keep Amy in the loop. Then throwing back her head, the mask's yellow beak stabbing the sky, she opened her mouth and let out a long, ragged screech.

'What are you doing?' Amy whispered through clenched teeth.

'Just copy me,' said Zed. 'Do everything I do.' And she squawked again.

Amy joined in, and the cormorants screeched back.

Zed moved to the edge of the water and the birds went quiet. Several skipped to the side, to get out of her way and they watched in silence as she kneeled down, leaned forward and put her hands in the river to wash them. Then cupping the water, she raised it to her mouth and drank.

One by one the cormorants also moved towards the river and dipped their heads down to drink, but then they took another couple of steps forward and slid their bodies into the water, ducking under the surface for just a moment before shuffling back out onto the sand. Zed looked at Amy. It seemed that hand washing just wasn't going to cut it. So together they, too, walked into the river. Luckily it wasn't deep enough for them to immerse themselves completely and their masks would not have survived a drenching, but they splashed water all over their bodies before stepping back onto the sandbank. That seemed to satisfy the cormorants and they were ready to begin.

Almost in a trance now, Zed walked slowly back towards the fire. Amy followed and the cormorants took up the same positions as before, surrounding the girls in an almost perfect circle. Then, one by one, they unfolded their wings, spreading their feathers so that instead of the boomerang blocks of black, it seemed to Zed that they were shaking out large black velvet gloves. They beat the air and in the middle of the circle, the wafts of oxygen revived the fire. The girls too, shook out their arms, the long sleeves of Zed's sweatshirt flapping up and down. The flames crackled, amber and tangerine, competing with the colours in the sky.

A large cormorant stepped forward and slowed the beat of its wings to a gentle flutter, retracting them slightly and shuffling forward, so that when the others followed suit, they closed up the circle into one long repeat pattern, like a concertina paper cut-out, linked by the tips of their wings and silhouetted against the dying sun.

Zed reached into her rucksack and pulled out a heavy, damp bag of raw fish. She gestured for Amy to unwrap their cooked mackerel and bring it back into the centre of the circle while she walked around the edge, in front of the birds, laying their offerings in the sand. Zed kneeled down and taking her portion onto her lap, she scraped off the blackened scaly skin and then peeled a chunk of the pale grey flesh away from the bones. She placed it in her mouth and began to chew. Amy did the same, and if she pulled a face no one could see it behind the mask. A few moments later the first of the birds bowed down and delicately, as if using chopsticks, picked up the whole fish in its beak and flicked its head back, so that its mouth and throat were all in a straight line. A series of twists and shudders and it swallowed the fish whole. The other birds joined in the feast.

And so it was time – for at least some words. Words the cormorants might not understand in themselves, but Zed hoped that if she delivered them with passion and conviction, their meaning would be understood. The sun was low now, and in a spillage of liquid copper, was seeping through the trees. She reached for the yeast starter and held up the jar towards the last of the light.

'We know that in the past, we have failed you.' Zed stopped. That wasn't right. The story of Gawen and Kerra was in the past, the story of the great cull was in the past, but there would be different stories happening now, somewhere in the world there would be some new betrayal. She took a deep breath and started again.

'We know that humans have harmed and continue to harm you.'

She looked at the cormorants and cleared her throat. The cormorants looked at her.

'But we pledge ourselves to help to heal and strengthen the bond between humans and the natural world. This is our home and your home.'

The bird who had eaten first threw back its head and let out a guttural cry. Immediately this was taken up by the others, who shrieked and grunted. Zed waited for the sound to die down before continuing,

'And from this day forward we will all live in harmony. We promise to live peacefully alongside you, and we'll encourage others to do so too. We–'

But she didn't need to say more. The squawking had erupted again, louder this time, and it didn't stop. Instead, as the volume increased, they flapped their wings, lifting up off the ground for a moment or two before landing again and bumping and butting each other for a place on the sandbank. No longer in a circle, they were skipping, hopping and dancing in and out of each other, getting closer and closer to the girls. Zed felt the panic rise again and she forgot that she was still holding the jar of yeast until suddenly, one of the birds leaped up into the air beside her, beating its wings and hovering by her shoulder. She flinched and just managed to swallow her scream when it dipped its head and then, very gently, tapped the glass, once, twice, with its beak. Was it the last of the light? Zed could have sworn that she saw a flash and for just a moment the jar, the chalice, glowed. The cormorant pumped its wings again, thrust out its legs and skidded back down to the ground behind her. Zed looked at the jar and then looked at Amy who had pushed back her mask and was grinning from ear to ear.

Zed hesitated for a moment, but with all the squawking and flapping, she thought, *why not?* and stumbled towards her sister, whooped, and gave her a high five.

The noise began to die down when Zed went over to the branches and untied the first of the origami cormorants. She kneeled down on the sand, cupping the bird and gently placed it onto the water.

The moon had appeared on the other side of the river, a large opal, hovering above the charcoal-grey trees. The birds settled and watched as Amy joined her sister with a second paper bird and then, one by one, they set them all free.

The tide was rising now and the sandbank shrinking. The paper birds were swiftly carried upstream towards Tremarrak and the cormorants began to follow. Some launched themselves into the water, soundlessly gliding away, and others took off from the narrow strip of sand, their wings thumping the air.

'*Benna sywes,*' Zed called out after them.

Amy raised an eyebrow.

'It means *may blessings follow.*'

'*Benna sywes,*' they both called out together.

Only one bird was left. It watched from the edge of the water as Amy and Zed began to roll up their damp trousers in preparation for wading back to the riverbank. As Amy packed up the rucksack, Zed got up from the sand and turned towards it.

'Kerra?' she said.

The cormorant blinked and took a few steps forward, away from the encroaching river. She tipped up her beak and squawked, swallowed and squawked again, but it was less abrasive this time, less guttural, and then the sound was softer, cleaner, and more like – yes, that was it, more like a vowel sound. A long *oooo*, followed by an *aaaaa* and an *eeee* and then she stopped, swallowed again and turned her head, in a series of little jerks, to look at the fire. Zed, too, turned towards the flames.

And then – a voice. The harshness was completely gone, but so was the volume, it was an echo again, like the first time Zed heard it.

'The song–'

The cormorant turned her head to look at Zed, and in between the heavy blinks, her eyes were filled with fire, green replaced with reflected orange flames.

'The song–' she said again.

Zed took a deep breath and began. She started slowly and sang a couple of lines by herself before she heard the harmony coming in and gliding along above the tune. And then, something else, something new, happened halfway through the second verse. Zed turned to look at Amy. Had she heard her practising? Had she picked up the melody? But no, Amy had taken off her mask and was lying back on the sand, her eyes and mouth firmly shut. It was a very quiet sound, just a kind of vibration to start with, deep and low, but it filled out into something more. *There* – it was definitely a voice now. A male voice, singing alongside her. It got louder, and the harmony soared as if pulling, pulling at the melody, willing it to lift itself too–

And Zed knew she wasn't needed anymore. She stopped singing and listened to the tune unfold and shift from melancholic to something joyous – something free.

The song ended and the cormorant turned, nodded then pushed herself out, low into the water. Only the tips of her tail feathers, the top angle of her wings and her long neck could be seen above the rushing river. She turned once more to look back at Zed, then with a little shudder, two great wings rose up out of the water and she took off, her trailing feet leaving a line of skimming stone splashes. Moments later, a flattened *M* crossed the sky, throbbing against the battered, pale yellow moon.

'Wow,' Amy cooed as the bird flew over her head.

'I think we're done here,' said Zed.

Thirty Five

Dad came home two days later. He'd delivered his presentation on the Pisa trip, then driven through the night and when he arrived, he came straight into the kitchen, dropped his bag and opened his arms to give Zed a hug.

'Sit down!' she ordered.

He did as he was told.

'Right, so every day is a fresh start, Dad!' she said, trying not to sound too sarcastic, 'and that's why we should always begin with a nutritious, tasty breakfast.' With a flourish she placed a rather flat, sort of roundish roll in front him on the table.

'Marmite and Cheesestrings,' she said proudly.

He stared at it.

'I made it myself,' she added.

'Well, it smells good,' he replied, picking it up. 'A little dense, perhaps.'

She *had* been rather heavy on the Cheesestrings and definitely didn't leave it long enough to rise.

Can't risk being asked to help out on a regular basis!

Dad drank some coffee and said he was off to see Mum at the hospital.

'Take some for her too!' said Zed, wrapping another lopsided roll in clingfilm.

'Really?' said Dad rather dubiously. 'She hasn't got much of an appetite.'

'Just get her to try it. One mouthful.'

'Haven't I forced enough bread on her?'

'I'll message her. Say it's from me. She'll try it then.'

'If you say so.'

'It's got to be better than hospital food!'

'Um – I'm not sure about that,' he replied.

That evening he insisted on sitting down for a proper talk with the girls.

'I'm not going away again,' he began. 'Part of us being in Cornwall is me not being away and I realised that when I was – you know, away.'

Amy smirked behind her fringe.

'And, here's the thing, I know that we've made the right choice, coming here. I guess, the whole stress of moving, all the changes – I don't know – I had a bit of a wobble back there, but I'm going to get us back on track, I promise.'

'Sounds good,' said Zed.

'I'm going to sort out things with your mum. And she's also going to try some different approaches, when she gets low. Not just loading up on pills and booze to get through the day.'

'Bring it on,' said Amy.

'And you're doing pretty well at sorting yourself out,' he said, patting Amy on the shoulder.

'And I know you've had a tough time, Zed,' he said, tugging on her plait, 'and I know you've been a bit lost in the mix, but all that's going to change. I'm going to be here for you girls. Both of you. Not in your face, I promise. Just be available if you need–'

'A lift somewhere?' said Amy. 'Although I'm thinking driving lessons are going to be pretty essential, living here. And maybe a car–'

'Yes, Mum and I have discussed that too.'

And somehow, in return for building him a website for the bakery, Amy got Dad to agree to buy her a new camera too.

Not a bad afternoon's work.

The following morning Mum rang from the hospital. She'd seen the doctor and was being discharged. Dad went to get her straight away. When they got back, they couldn't stop fussing around each other. Dad spent the first ten minutes trying to tuck Mum into an armchair and then she got up almost immediately and limped up the stairs to run him a bath. Amy just rolled her eyes and left them to it, but Zed was watching carefully.

Maybe blessed yeast was making a difference.

She went down to the boathouse and got the kayak out. And it felt okay. She planned to drift down river into Clewmor, see how things were in town and maybe buy another postcard to send to Beth who'd finally left her a long voice message. Zed knew she should return the call, be the bigger person here, and actually talk to her, but she couldn't face it – not yet anyway. Caitlin had also called. Zed had rung her straight back, but it had gone to voicemail. Maybe she'd send her some fudge. Caitlin loved fudge and she'd need cheering up – third wheeling was going to be tough!

Zed was finally getting the hang of the tides, but she was still taken by surprise at the speed of the current. In no time at all she could see the china clay docks and the church steeple, and she was just approaching the bend in the river, when she heard a shout and looked over to the bank. It was Denzil, not exactly waving, but beating his arms up and down like he was shaking out a rug. He was fishing off a small wooden pontoon. Behind him, a thin strip of grass stretched between a wonky stone cottage and the water's edge. Zed did a big loop and paddled upstream. As she got closer, she saw crab pots, big plastic buoys and thick coils of rope all piled up by the back door. The door itself and all the window frames were painted bright yellow.

'Where have you been?'

''Round an' about.'

'Tamsin was looking for you.'

'When?'

'Couple of days ago.'

'W...w...wen' up country. Me mum sent some money an' that. I thought maybe it would be n-nice to see her. She'd sent an address, see?'

'Oh, right, well, that's good.'

'Didn't get any further than Exeter though, b-b-bit of an altercation, en route!'

'Oh.'

'Yeah, well, I'm not at my b-best in crowds, or in cities for that matter. Always knew B-B-Bristol might be a challenge!'

'So you came back?'

'Was thrown off the t-t-train. An' it took a day or two to sort meself out.'

'Is this where you're living?' Zed asked looking up at the cottage.

'Yeah, I stay 'ere s...s...sometimes. Where are you goin'?'

'I'm going into Clewmor.'

'Meetin' up with your friends?' he said, switching the rod from one hand to the other as he lifted and shook out each arm.

'I don't have any friends, do I? Well I do back home, obviously, but not down here.'

'What about my s...s...sister?' He didn't wait for an answer. 'An' you'll be makin' some more when you s...s...start school.'

'Maybe – but what if they don't like me?' Zed blurted out.

'Go on! What if you don't like them, more like. That's what you be thinkin'!'

'Well, yes. That too.'

Denzil chuckled.

'Come on,' he said. 'Tie 'er up! You must be thirsty in this heat! How about you try a bit of c...cider? I made it meself for the weekend. It's s...strong though, so just a drop.'

'Um, well maybe some water,' said Zed, concentrating on climbing out of the boat without capsizing it. It wasn't easy. And she wasn't sure how stable the pontoon was either.

'Water? You're soft in the head if you choose water over me apples. You'll be s...soft in the head, mind, if you choose me apples!'

He handed her a flask. 'It's a good batch, this lot,' he said, fiddling with his beard.

Zed cautiously unscrewed the lid and – whoa! The fumes were enough, but she took a tiny sip. She expected bubbles, but it was flat, thick and smoky. She could taste ginger, cinnamon, apples (obviously!) and it had a strange bitterness, actually more like a burning at the end. She screwed up her face and Denzil threw back his head and laughed. A great big belly laugh. She couldn't help laughing too.

''Ere, you'll be fine, maid, if you decide to be. See, it's like I told you before, there's a lot you can take from them b-birds.'

'The cormorants?' said Zed.

'Yes, the cormorants. They'll learn you all sorts. Look 'ere, you got the life you 'ad up there an' those friends aren't goin' anywhere, but you've gotta m... make a new life down 'ere too. Commit to it, like the cormorants when they dive for their food. They s...s...submerge themselves in the water and for that moment, when they be in the water, they're not a bird, but a fish, see?'

'I'm not sure I do,' said Zed.

'They can be bird, one minute, an' like a fish another, but when they be a bird, they be a bird an' when they be a fish, they're a fish. An' when they be a fish, fishin', you can guarantee that's all they're thinkin' about. Not feelin' sad that b-backalong they were a bird.'

'Okay,' said Zed. 'I think.'

'That's commitment to the m...moment. An' you should do the same! Not comparin' new life with old, an' new friends with old, but really givin' yourself to life 'ere, now you're 'ere.'

'Okay – I get it.'

But Denzil hadn't finished.

'You need to plan a bit too. That's what them birds do. Them feathers aren't waterproof, they've got no oil in 'em, so they 'ave to soak 'em before divin' to lose their b-b-buoyancy. Those birds couldn't fish if they bleddy floated.'

'I don't see how–'

'Get out there! Don't wait for it to 'appen. Make it 'appen! Then there'll be nothin' to worry 'bout.' With that, he dipped his chin and scooped his head down towards the water.

Zed thought about this for a moment.

'What you doin' on Saturday then? You c-comin' to the Mussel Fest?'

'I don't know. What is it?' asked Zed.

''It's in Clewmor. 'Appens ev'ry year. There be all sorts of food stalls, cookin' demonstrations, bit of singin' an' the like. You never know, I m...might even go along and share a bit of me cider. Then, if it's so important to you,' he said with a shrug, 'you could make some friends b-before school starts!'

'I'll see,' said Zed. 'Look, before I get back in the boat, can I use your – do you have a loo?'

'That's what the b-b-bushes are for!'

'Yes, right, of course. I think I'll leave it then.'

But he was laughing again. 'G-got you, din' I?' he said. 'It's through the back of the kitchen.'

When she came out, he was still chuckling to himself. She ignored him and climbed back into the kayak.

'Plannin' an' commitment,' said Denzil, waving a finger at her.

'Yeah – yeah,' said Zed. 'I'm on it.'

Thirty Six

Dad had got the oven started again.

'Can't think why I was struggling,' he said. 'It's going like a dream.'

'And what gastronomic delights will we be sampling today?' asked Mum.

'Well,' said Dad, beaming. 'You have a choice. I've been plotting with Cordelia and we thought we'd try something with her goat's cheese. I'm thinking a rye with tarragon, or no, maybe a rye with goat's cheese and thyme. That should be pretty spectacular.'

'Ugh! Goat's cheese,' said Amy, 'that's rank! It'll taste like rotting socks!'

'I want to have another go at a rustic cider bread too. The Yarg worked a treat, but it needs more oomph.'

'Well, if you want cider with a punch,' said Zed, 'I know just the man for job.'

Zed had messaged Tamsin to say Denzil was staying in the little yellow cottage down on the water. Tamsin messaged back saying she was going over to see him later that afternoon.

> *Dad would love to try some of his cider do you reckon he'd come over if I invited him?*

> *Who knows! What's with inviting him round to meet your parents before me???*

> *You can come too!*

> *When?*

> *Tomorrow eve?*

Busy. Got Aikido.
Then immediately another ping and–

Why don't we meet up tonight? I could come over after I see my bro. Meet at boathouse?

Cordelia came over for a tasting session. Everyone sat around the table and Dad brought in four warm crusty loaves. The bread he'd made with her cheese was a meal in itself: rich, tangy and utterly delicious. And they all agreed, except Amy of course, who said she'd rather stick pins in her eyes than try it, that thyme was the way to go.

'Will you make some for the Mussel Fest?' Zed asked. 'Will you make lots?'

'Yes, we'll take some into town on Saturday,' replied Dad.

'And I invited Denzil over for tomorrow,' Zed added.

'Did you now?' said Cordelia under her breath.

'Not sure he'll come, but I asked him to bring some of his cider for Dad's bread.'

Cordelia grunted.

'Are you actually going to have like a proper stall, then?' said Amy, looking at one of the flyers Zed had picked up in town.

'Looks like it,' said Dad. 'Madam here went and booked it, so I don't have much choice.'

'Now,' said Cordelia, leaning forward onto the table to push herself up out of her chair, 'have you got enough yeast? I could give you some more if you're running low–'

'No!' Zed yelled.

Everyone looked at her.

'Steady on,' said Dad.

'Sorry – it's just – it's really important that–' Zed took a moment and then said, 'I've taken ours out of the fridge and I've been feeding it regularly. And it's ready. It's perfect and there's plenty of it.'

She glared at Amy, hoping for a bit of back up.

'Okay – if you say so,' said Dad, glancing at Mum.

'I do!' said Zed. 'And you have to promise. Do you promise to use it?'

'If you keep on adding flour and water, like I showed you, you can use that one forever,' said Cordelia.

Dad sat back and looked at Zed. 'You are a funny girl!'

'Do you promise, Dad? Please. Do you promise?'

'Okay, okay. Of course!' he said. 'I promise.'

'And while we're on the subject of baking,' said Zed, turning to Cordelia, 'can you give me your recipe for apple cake? You know, the bready one you made for my birthday?'

'Of course.'

'Wait, it needs yeast, right?'

'Yes – yes, it does.'

'Perfect.'

When Zed set off for the boathouse that evening, she thought of Kerra, all those years ago, skipping down to the river to meet Gawen. And the lightness she felt walking under the viaduct wasn't just about not carrying a hockey stick, fencing vest, stiff biker jacket and helmet – in fact she was carrying speakers for her music and a picnic basket that Cordelia had packed up with goat's cheese straws, chutney and elderflower fizz and that was actually quite heavy – but something had shifted. She had little butterflies for sure, like the blue ones chasing each other in circles down in the long grass, but she kept them at bay by repeating Denzil's words over and over again.

Don't wait for it to 'appen. Make it 'appen! Then there'll be nothin' to worry 'bout.

Cordelia had given her a tartan rug to take too.

'It's going to be a lovely clear night,' she'd said. 'Make the most of it!'

Zed waited outside for a bit. She left the basket on the path and edged her way down the slip, took off her shoes and sat with her toes in the water. There wasn't a cloud in the sky, but when the sun dropped behind the trees and the warmth of the day began to recede, she stood up, dried off her feet in the long grass and went around to open the door.

She'd brought down all the tea lights left over from the séance. She lit them and placed them along the windowsill. Then she lit the stove, put on some very mellow music – a playlist Caitlin had made for them all when they were stressing about exams – folded the blanket in half and sat on it, crossed-legged and lulled by the flames flickering behind the soot-streaked glass.

She didn't hear Tamsin arrive on her bike (another advantage of well-oiled brakes!), nor come into the boathouse, but when Zed got pins and needles and stood up to shake out her leg, Tamsin was standing behind her and they stared at each other in the mirror.

'Nice vibe in here,' Tamsin whispered. She was close enough for the words to tickle Zed's ear and send a shot of liquid heat all the through her body.

Keep breathing. Keep breathing.

Zed reached up to touch Tamsin's face and turn it towards her. It was quite something to be standing so close, to feel the warmth of her body after her bike ride and see that flawless skin, the downy pink of her earlobes and the tip of her tongue as she licked her finger and lifted it up to her–

'What is that thing you do with your eyebrows?'

'Sorry – I know – I'm smoothing them down.'

'Why?'

''Cause they're sort of bushy, like those fat caterpillars!'

'They're perfect – and real! Not plucked out and then pencilled back, I mean what is that all about?'

'I think I do it when I'm nervous.'

'So – Cordelia told you about this place, right?'

'Yeah. A few days ago. She'd never really talked about it before, when it was all locked up, I mean.'

'And its history scares you?'

'It does,' Tamsin said, 'but not for the reasons you think.'

'Okaay?'

'It's not the ghoulish stuff that freaks me out, you know, dead people, dead birds – it's kinda the stuff before.'

'You've lost me.'

Tamsin swallowed. 'So girls are my thing, I've known that for a while an' I'm guessing you know that too. I mean that that's what I'm into and I'm really hoping that maybe you – anyway, look, I'm out there an' cool with it and my friends are cool with it and I've played around a bit, but this – this feels different.' She hesitated for a moment then turned to brush Zed's hand with her lips. 'Being here with you feels different and, yeah, that is kinda scary.'

'Because it's a place where two sweet, hot young things fell in love?' said Zed with a wink. A kind of wobbly wink, she couldn't really control any of the muscles in her face.

Tamsin grinned. 'The way Cordelia talks about it, and we're reading between the lines here obviously, Gawen and Kerra could hardly keep their hands off each other.'

'Well, this is all a bit scary for me too,' said Zed slowly, 'but I've been more scared, and I'm still here.'

'So, does that mean–?'

'Just kiss me.'

And they did. Kiss. And the kissing went on and on until Zed's lips felt sore, bruised even, not that she cared. When the fire died down, they took the blanket outside and lay in each other's arms. They kissed some more and then rolled onto their backs and gazed up at the sky. Zed had never seen so much shimmering light. City lights, yes, streets and streets of yellow and white, the flashing red brake lights, the dazzling blue and green on the top of the skyscrapers in the distance, but a sky like this? Filled with thousands and thousands of luminous stars?

It was literally, right up there.

Thirty Seven

Mum and Dad spent the whole of the following day up in the bakery. Talking. Zed wandered up in that direction a few times, just to check that she couldn't hear any shouting, banging pots, or slamming doors, but no – she could hear voices, they were definitely having a pretty animated conversation, but it wasn't loud enough for her to listen in, which was probably a good thing.

They hadn't come back down when, at six o'clock on the dot, Denzil came trudging through the field at the bottom of the garden, over the little wooden bridge and across the lawn. He was carrying four large glass bottles of cider, two in each hand, and he passed them to Zed with a grunt. Slung over his shoulder was a duffle bag full of sketchbooks. When he sat on the step to take off his boots, Zed noticed that he'd trimmed his beard.

'These are for you,' he said, looking at the ground, but holding out the duffle bag to Amy. 'Thought you might be w...w...wantin' to see 'em.'

'Sure, um, why not?' said Amy, catching Zed's eye and raising her eyebrows.

'It's good to meet you,' said Dad, coming through the door with Mum and pouring the cider into glass tankards without delay. 'It seems you've got my daughter into bird watching!'

'Ha!' said Denzil. 'I reckon they be the ones w...watchin' us!'

'Quite right!' said Dad.

He looked at Mum, who smiled and shook her head, then handed a tankard to Denzil. Dad raised his to his lips, took a long slurp, swallowed, shut his eyes, and grinned.

'Now that,' he said, 'is pretty special.'

And they were off. Denzil told Dad how to fish for sea bass, the best creeks to go foraging for samphire and where the edible mushrooms grew in Tremelin Woods. Dad told Denzil how to make wild garlic pesto, how to avoid the hassle of pricking sloes and how easy it was to pop the breasts out of a dead pheasant and save yourself all that plucking.

Amy sat down on the sofa and started flicking through Denzil's sketchbooks.

'These are epic,' she said.

'Let's see,' said Mum, peering over her shoulder.

'I mean, the sketches are, they're really awesome, but the birds, those birds, are something else.'

'That's what I've been tellin' your s...s...sister,' said Denzil, beaming.

'I want to photograph them,' said Amy. 'I want to do some kind of project documenting their life here on the river, but not just some boring wildlife photography thing – I'm not interested in pretty pictures, I want to really get at their characters, their intelligence–'

'Well, I can show you the best places to see 'em,' said Denzil.

'Maybe even explore the way they've interacted with humans, over the years,' she winked at Zed, 'and the ambiguity of that relationship.'

'You do it,' said Denzil, 'and I've no doubt it's a story worth tellin'!'

'Thing is, I just need to get my new camera.'

Amy looked demurely at Dad. Well, it was the best she could do. It's fair to say demure was always going to be a challenge.

'I was sayin' to Zed the other day, folks over Tremarrak way 'ave been naggin' me for ages to 'ave a little exhibition in the l-l-library. Nice little gallery, they got up there too,' said Denzil.

'We could do it together!' said Amy, bouncing up and down on the sofa. 'Your drawings and my photographs.'

'Whooahh!' said Zed, 'that's some serious gate-crashing Ames!'

Denzil's shoulders twitched and he pulled the little tuft on his chin.

'I wonder if they'd have space for a jewellery cabinet?' said Mum. 'I'd love to try making some little painted eggs, maybe as earrings; they're such a marvellous colour. And the shape of the bird, the wings and the neck. It's such a strong outline. I'm thinking I could work up something in silver.'

'Hold your horses! You don't even have any photos yet!' said Dad, looking at Amy. 'And as for you–' he continued, turning to Mum and shaking his head.

Mum, Amy and Zed all stopped and stared at him.

'What?'

No one said anything.

'Well–' he spluttered. 'This young man has been *invited* to show his stuff! What's more, you're talking exhibitions and neither of you have even begun to make anything. Amy hasn't got a decent camera yet and as far as I know you've barely opened your toolbox since we've been here.'

'Is it me, or is that just a bit hypocritical?' said Mum after a long pause.

Denzil had raised his hand to his mouth and started rocking back and forward banging his finger on his lips.

'Talking the talk, before walking the walk, eh Dad?' said Zed with a nervous giggle. 'Whatever next?'

Dad went very quiet and looked into his empty glass. Mum and Amy went very quiet and looked at Denzil.

Denzil lurched forwards, shook out his hands and cocked his head at Dad.

'You'll be needin' a t-t-top up,' he said.

When they'd finished the cider and they'd soaked it up with yet more bread, Denzil got up out of his chair.

'I'll bring you another b-bottle tomorrow for them Yarg loaves,' he said.

'Why don't you leave behind the one in the duffle bag?' suggested Amy.

'Eh?' muttered Denzil. 'Ah, um – well, I'm thinkin', maybe that one is for someone else. I was gonna ask one of you to leave it on the step across the road.' He looked at Zed. 'Just as I'm up in this direction an' 'aven't been for a while–'

'Why don't you take it across yourself?' asked Zed.

'No, no, that wouldn't be a good idea. She can be proper teasy! You do it an' I'll be on me way.' He looked out across the lawn into the pitch black of the bushes. 'Though, maybe I'll risk the lanes this time.'

He asked Mum not to turn on the outside lamp and after he'd said goodnight, Zed took him around the side of the house to the road. He would have made it, but the gate gave him away, squeaking as it dragged across the pebbles. On went the light in Cordelia's porch.

'Oh bleddy hell!' he muttered as her door opened just enough for Buttons to barge through and charge across the road, jumping up at him and yapping joyfully.

'Someone's pleased to see you,' said a stony voice.

''Ere–' said Denzil, snatching the cider from Zed and holding it out to Cordelia. 'You can't argue with the c-colour of that!'

He didn't wait for her to take it, just placed it on top of her vegetable rack and trudged off into the darkness.

Thirty Eight

On Saturday morning, Dad was up at four o'clock baking bread. Zed knew this because she had woken at four o'clock too. And at three o'clock. And at two...

By eight-thirty he was making his third trip down to the boathouse, with baskets of freshly baked crusty loaves and rolls piled up in Cordelia's wheelbarrow. He was determined to go into Clewmor by the river and the stalls had been set up on the town quay, so it made more sense than trying to drive his new van down through the narrow one-way streets. Mum said that if he was going to arrive by boat, he had to dress it and she and Cordelia had sat up until midnight making bunting. On each triangular flag they'd sewn either a loaf of bread or a yellow saffron bun, studded with currants.

Amy had been nagging him to come up with a name, so that she could at least buy a domain for the website, get him an email address and design a holding page, but he was far too busy fine-tuning his recipes.

'It will come to me,' he kept saying, 'when I'm not thinking about it.' And it did, apparently, when he was pushing the empty wheelbarrow back along the path, its wheels trundling over the uneven ground.

'*Roots!*' he yelled at Mum as he came into the kitchen. She was making a flask of coffee to take on the boat.

'Yes?' answered Zed, finishing her breakfast.

'*Roots.*'

'Are you for real?' said Amy. She'd managed to drag herself out of bed, down the stairs and into the kitchen, and was moving around like a zombie, but it seemed that her cognitive function was pretty sharp, she'd got there way before Zed.

'It's taken you all week to come up with that?'

'It's perfect.'

'Yeah right. Really inspired, Dad!'

'It's our name.'

'Yeah, but it sounds like you're selling vegetables!' said Mum.

'And it's our culture. It's about what we stand for. It's about going back to basics, back to the earth. It's about us putting down roots with every friend we make, every exchange of produce or recipes, every shared ideal or gesture of mutual respect. It's about connecting to the land, to this place, our home. It's about–'

'If that's a marketing strap line, it's not exactly catchy.'

'But it'll be good for the website and that's where you come in. So you'd better start taking notes!'

'Is Cordelia coming with us?' asked Mum.

'No,' said Dad.

'Why not?' said Zed. 'She has to!'

'I don't think she's that keen on boats.'

'But she's coming, right? Later?'

'I don't know – I think so. Maybe she's getting a lift in with Dicky Glynn.'

'She has to come!' said Zed. 'It's super important that she's there. You know what? I'm just going to check–' and she was off across the lane.

Zed put on her new shorts and a little tank top and then changed into a dress and then her dungarees, and then her dress again and then the shorts with a different top. She picked up her sunglasses and a notebook from her desk and went out onto the landing. Even Amy had to admit it was going to be too hot for jeans and for the first time in like, ever, she wore a little denim dress and some platform sandals.

'Nice,' said Zed, as they walked down the stairs together.

'Looking pretty buff, yourself!' was Amy's reply.

As they set off downriver in the boat, an egg yolk sun trembled in the sky. It was a bit of a squeeze, the four of them and the baskets of bread, and the boat sat fairly low in the water, but the river was flat and calm; a shimmering, silver ribbon, stretching out behind them all the way back to Tremarrak, with its solar panelled roofs and windows flashing like paparazzi cameras. Ahead, the broad metallic strip pushed back against the riverbanks, with their double layers of trees, real and reflected, until the sky was the backdrop, Clewmor and Penkerris were the painted wings, and the blue water was centre stage. A stage where the sunlight dazzled and made diamonds.

Perhaps there are spriggans swimming...

Zed could hear music by the time they got to Denzil's cottage and as they chugged passed the first of the pontoons in the harbour, she could see smoke rising from big flat pans of paella being cooked on the beach below the yacht club. The smell wafted out to the boat. Chicken, chorizo, and the fishy whiff of mussels and prawns. Dad shut his eyes, breathed in and lifted his face to the sun, as if that was the source of the delicious aroma. *I guess if you're a big picture kind of guy,* thought Zed, *then it is.*

As the boat zigzagged in and out of the buoys, they could see a crowd on the town quay, gathered around a small stage where the first of the cookery demonstrations was taking place. Dad steered as close to the beach as he could, and when the hull ground to a halt against the sand, he rolled up his trousers, jumped out and lifted Mum over to the harbour steps. Amy and Zed were able to leap onto a dry bit of rock, the first of several stepping stones. Wading back through the water, Dad grabbed the painter, slung it over his shoulder and dragged the boat up onto the dry shingle near the wall.

'We never found out what her name was, did we?' he said, tying the rope to a metal ring on the post by the harbour steps.

'What, the boat?' said Mum.

'Let's call her *Eve*,' said Zed.

'Well, that's as good a name as any,' said Dad. '*Eve* it is.'

The stalls were a series of trestle tables laid with blue and white striped cloth. All they needed to do was lift up their baskets and they were good to go. There were little knobbly granary rolls and brown crusty loaves dusted with flour. The rye bread was topped with oozing soft white goat's cheese and stuffed with sprigs of thyme and the lumps of nut and spiky rosemary in the shiny crust of the walnut bread glistened in the sunshine. As Zed set out the slabs of pepper cake, she could smell the rich christmassy spices, ginger and cinnamon, almost overwhelming in the heat. She put a lemon cake at the far end of table, so its cleaner fragrance wouldn't compete.

Zed recognised Doreen laying out jams and chutneys next to them and on the other side of her someone was selling big wheels of Cornish Blue cheese. Under an awning attached to the side of the pub, there were lots of fish laid out on rapidly melting ice, squid with their translucent tentacles and large terracotta coloured crabs.

Denzil was outside the British Legion, hopping from one foot to the other and nodding at a tall guy with a deep suntan, a head full of bouncy blond dreadlocks and a real twinkle in his eye. They were taking it in turns to stir a huge vat of fish stew and scoop it into polystyrene pint cups. Already a queue was reaching right around the corner. Everyone was chattering and laughing though, and no one seemed in the slightest bit put out by the wait. And then Zed saw why. In between handing out the stew, Denzil was darting in and out of the queue with a tray of his cider, giving out fairly large samples to anyone who'd take them. Amy sauntered over to him and picked up two. He grinned at her.

'How's it going?' she said.

'Not b-bad!'

'You want to introduce me to your friend?'

Zed told Dad that today wasn't so much about selling his loaves as getting as many people to try them as possible, even those who had tried them before – in fact, especially those that had tried them before! He looked a bit confused.

'Just trust me on this,' she said. 'A lot has happened since then!'

He ripped some open, put them in a basket and left Mum and Zed to mind the stall while he worked his way around the quay, talking to anyone who was interested including other stallholders, musicians, shopkeepers, publicans and the cooks waiting for their turn to get up on the stage. One of them recommended Dad's bread to mop up any smears of his smoked haddock chowder and it turned out he was quite a well-known TV chef. Luckily Amy captured it all on her phone.

And that wasn't all she photographed. She took close-up photos of the Morris dancers' feet, all blurs and streaks of ribbon, and tables of empty glasses twinkling in the sunlight. She found an ice cream melting, merging pink and brown as it pooled in the gutter, and a mound of inky blue mussel shells, some clamped shut and some opened out and empty, but still hinged together like pearly grey butterfly wings.

A male voice choir had started singing sea shanties by the war memorial. They were collecting for the new church roof. Mum left Zed to watch the bread and she went over to listen and got chatting to a potter who lived up at the top of the hill.

Dad kept coming back to refill his basket. He was bouncing from foot to foot and rubbing the top of his head.

'They're going like–'

'Hot cakes?' said Zed.

'Yep. That's the one!' said Dad. 'Even the man who was so rude about them last time, you remember?'

'That's Mr Cardew you were talking to!' said Doreen, leaning across the table towards them. 'Even if you remember, he won't! He's definitely losing his marbles.'

'I've been chatting to the chef at Clewmor Hall again,' Dad said. 'They're re-opening next week and he loved the rye bread! The Lugger and The Harbourside Café both want to put in an order. And there is a woman I was talking to from

Penkerris who wants to try selling them in the village shop over there.'

'Mrs Penprase?' said Doreen.

'Have you spoken to the guy that helms the ferry?' said Zed. 'Maybe give him one to try and tell him he can have some freebies if he takes them across?'

'Yes, Pete will never say *no* to anything edible,' said Doreen. 'He adores my jam! He's over there, look, been off work recently, so it's nice to see him out and about!'

'Mmm – I think we met before,' said Dad as he set off with his basket.

'Who's the guy who runs the fish and chip shop?' Zed asked Doreen.

'Why, are you thinkin' of buying it? He's over there too, singing with the choir.'

'Can you mind the stall for just a moment?'

'Yes, of course, you take your time.'

And there was Cordelia. She was sitting with Buttons on the bottom step of the war memorial, wearing a battered straw hat and a faded floral dress, which she kept smoothing over her knees. Zed was working her way towards her, stopping to give rolls to everyone she passed, even the occasional seagull. Well, no one noticed and special circumstances and all that. When Zed got closer, she saw that Cordelia was talking to Denzil, her head on one side, hiding her expression in the shade of her hat. Then she reached up to take a cup of cider from his tray and her chin followed the line of her arm, lifting her face into the sun – and she was smiling.

But then she stopped, squinted and said something. Denzil spun around looking eagerly at where she was pointing.

'M...Mum?' he yelled.

A tall, slim woman, her hair scraped back in a ponytail, was standing under the awning at the side of the pub. She held her hands to her face for a moment, as if she was praying, and then started running towards them. Well, she was trying to run, but she was carrying a rucksack and it was pretty bulky. Denzil shoved his tray of cider onto Cordelia's lap and stood twitching his shoulders and tugging at his chin. When she reached them, she stopped, wriggled her arms free of the straps and held them out.

She waited. And waited – until Denzil dipped his head and nestled it into her neck.

Zed could see the tray shaking as Cordelia put it down, and then slowly got to her feet. She stayed back until Denzil lifted his head and then hesitantly stepped forward herself. And Suki threw her arms around her grandmother.

The music and the dancing continued all afternoon, long after the last of the cooking demonstrations and the abandoned paella pans had been licked clean by two dogs on the beach, long after there was no beach and the abandoned pans were lifted up onto the quay to stop them floating away. And long after it was announced over the megaphone that a community that celebrated good food in such style deserved a decent chippy and it would be re-opening on Monday!

Mum and Dad went into one of the pubs with the potter and his girlfriend and Amy and Zed sat on the harbour wall with the basket of bread, looking out to sea and flicking though Amy's photos on her phone.

'Hey, Zed.'

She took a moment before looking up.

Yep, still gorgeous.

'Hi Tams.'

'Did you cycle in?'

'Nah, we came on the boat.' Zed pointed to Eve, bobbing about in the water by the steps.

'Sweet,' said Tamsin, smiling that smile. 'It's turning out to be quite a day. My mum's here!'

'I guessed as much,' said Zed, pointing over to Cordelia and Suki who were now sitting side by side on a hay bale and watching Denzil hopping around in front them and throwing his arms about. Cordelia didn't seem to entirely approve of his antics, but Suki was laughing and kept clapping her hands.

'She just rocked up. Good day to choose, huh?' said Tamsin.

'Yep, it's a perfect day to choose!' said Zed.

Tamsin glanced at Amy.

'Oh– so, this is my sister!'

'Hey,' said Tamsin, stuffing her hands into her pockets. 'Me an' Zed are gonna be in the same class.'

'Is that right?' said Amy. She was grinning in a way that made Zed want to punch her.

'You'll be with *them* too,' Tamsin pointed. 'Hey, Bella, come here.'

There were three girls sitting outside a café and eating iced berry lollies, laughing and pouting at each other with their red stained lips. One of them turned, waved, and then jumped up and ran over. She was wearing stripy leggings and a t-shirt that said: *I'm not weird, I'm limited edition.*

'Hello. Are you the bakers?'

'Are you the blogger?'

Bella grinned and said in a really bad American drawl, 'Shucks! You can't get away with nothin' in this town!' Then she added, 'But seriously, are you giving out those delicious buns?' She looked at Tamsin and winked.

Zed blushed.

'Well, my dad is trying, well no, I guess he is–' She took a breath. 'That's Amy and I'm Zed. We're actually the Roots and we live in Tremelin.'

'Zed?'

'As in the letter. The last letter.'

'It's short for Zoë,' said Amy.

'It's the first letter in the word zany – and zesty – and zealous and they're all pretty cool things to be,' said Bella.

'So is zen,' said Tamsin and she shut her eyes and pretended to meditate. Zed giggled.

'Zed is joining our year.'

'Yeah?'

'Yep, I'll be starting on Monday.'

'Hey, guys,' Bella yelled to the others. 'Say hi to Zed. She's friends with Tams!' They all turned this time and waved.

'Oh, um, hi, Mr Robinson,' said Bella as a tall, rather gaunt man smiled weakly at the girls and tried to get past.

'We hope you're, you know – feeling a bit better.'

'Thank you, Bella,' he said tightly.

'That's our science teacher,' Tamsin whispered to Zed. 'Remind me to tell you about him later.'

But Zed was already up and thrusting the basket of bread into his chest.

'Oh, um, would you like one of these?'

'No, thank you!'

'Please–'

He took a step back, frowned, and shook his head.

Zed reached into the basket, picked out a roll and waved it under his nose.

'Think of it as an experiment–'

'Really, I–'

'Smell it!'

He gingerly sniffed the bread.

'Now, you have to taste it.'

'No thank you,' he said again, but Zed didn't move.

'Wait!' She grabbed her phone out of her pocket and tapped the screen urgently.

Bella and Tamsin exchanged looks and Bella took Zed by the elbow and tried to steer her away, but she wasn't budging.

'What you can smell is fermentation, caramelisation and non-enzymatic Maillard reactions!'

'Well, yes, very good, young lady,' he said, looking at her properly for the first time.

'Go on, taste it!' she said again.

'Do I know you?'

'Not yet, but you will. Next term. Now just a mouthful – the tiniest taste–'

He sighed, nibbled the crust and Zed beamed at him and stood aside.

'I've read your blog,' Zed said to Bella. 'I'm sorry I only made it down to the beach for one clean up. We've been kind of busy, what with moving in and there was a bit of stuff, well, quite a lot of stuff to sort out.'

'No worries,' said Bella. 'I heard you'd been flat out!'

'I could come down next week though, after school?'

'No need. I mean, we're always up for volunteers, but the worst of the rubbish has stopped washing up, so we're all good again. At least for the time being.'

'Oh,' said Zed, sounding very disappointed.

Not cool.

'Come paddle boarding instead!' said Bella.

'And come tomorrow,' said Tamsin, 'we're having a party, to mark the end of the holidays. We'll do a cook-out and play volleyball an' stuff.'

'And she's pretty mean on the ukulele too. You should definitely come. Three o'clock. Bring something to eat, which I'm guessing won't be a problem, and drink. You too,' she said, nodding at Amy.

Tamsin caught Zed's eye and said quietly, 'You will come, won't you?'

'Of course I will!'

She smiled and Zed was pretty sure the pink in her cheeks wasn't sunburn.

'See you tomorrow then,' said Bella, heading back to join her friends.

'Yeah, see you on the beach,' said Tamsin, then she turned back, and gently brushed her fingers down Zed's arm. All the little hairs stood on end.

'Would you like to meet up first? Maybe you could come an' meet my mum an' then I could, um, take you there?' she said quietly.

Like a date?

Zed nodded and grinned. It was all she could manage.

And then Tamsin was off, skirting around the edge of the dancing and sliding into the crowd.

Amy elbowed Zed in the ribs.

'What?' said Zed, laughing. 'What?'

They went back to looking at the photographs. There was one of Dad twirling Mum as they danced past a man playing an accordion, and another of Buttons lying stretched out under a table, his tongue lolling out of the corner of his mouth and his body pressed up against the cool glass of an empty bottle. The next one showed Cordelia's squashed hat lying by a plate of sardines. In the one after, Cordelia was fanning herself, sitting next to Suki and sucking on a stick of rock. You could just make out Denzil's hand on her shoulder.

'Did you have anything to do with that?' said Amy.

'I might have done,' Zed whispered coyly.

'Thought you looked a bit pleased with yourself.'

'Well, I saw a postcard with her address on in Denzil's cottage and figured that maybe all she needed was a little nudge – and a parcel of her favourite cake!'

The last photo was of a line of people leaning over the harbour wall. They were watching the rescue of the paella pans, a row of bottoms, twisted torsos, sweaty, smiling faces side on, and pink arms pointing down towards the beach. There was so much movement, such a story unfolding beneath the big blue sky that Zed didn't notice them at first, in the distance, perfectly spaced and each one gaining height as if mounted above a mantelpiece. Three cormorants. She'd know that shape anywhere now; beaks, heads and necks drawn out into flat black felt-tipped lines. They were arrows with wings, like three wonky crosses, flying into the sun.

ABOUT THE AUTHOR

After working as an actor and arts administrator in London, Clare Owen married a boat builder and moved to Cornwall. She promptly had three children and set up an improvised theatre company, re-enacting the stories of their audiences around the county.
More recently she has co-written and performed with the all women ensemble, 'Riot of the Freelance Mind' and she regularly reads her short fiction at spoken word events and local festivals.

Arachne Press first published Clare with a short story *Cormorant,* which was part of 2018's *An Outbreak of Peace* anthology. As you might expect from the title, there is a link to the novel.

More Young Adult Books
from Arachne Press
arachnepress.com

Devilskein & Dearlove by Alex Smith
ISBN: 978-1-909208-15-5
NOMINATED FOR THE 2015 CILIP CARNEGIE MEDAL.
A young adult novel set in South Africa. Young Erin Dearlove has lost everything, and is living in a run-down apartment block in Cape Town. Then she has tea with Mr Devilskein, the demon who lives on the top floor, and opens a door into another world.

Brat: Book One of *The Naming of Brook Storyteller*
by Ghillian Potts
ISBN: 978-1-909208-41-4
On her twelfth birthday Brat's father disappears. She waits, but he never comes back. Reduced to begging and determined to find out what has happened to him, she is helped by Gray and Baylock, whom she quickly discovers are outlaws. Brat finds that nothing is simple, nowhere is safe, and being reunited with her family must wait, as more pressing tasks fall into her path.

Spellbinder: Book Two of *The Naming of Brook Storyteller*
by Ghillian Potts
ISBN: 978-1-909208-46-9
Brook, now called Spellbinder, is working as Remembrancer to her friend Graycat, now the Young Overlord Lady Quicksilver, when Storytellers start disappearing. Spellbinder is captured and forced to summon the Elder Dragons, but when she cannot control them, she must break her Storyteller vow and forfeit her most precious possession – her name.

Wolftalker, Book Three of *The Naming of Brook Storyteller*
by Ghillian Potts
ISBN: 978-1-909208-49-0
Someone is felling gilden trees, the life of the Overlord is threatened, and Storyteller Brook Wolftalker Dragonfriend (known as Brat to her friends) and her new apprentice Cricket, try to unravel who is behind the plot, and more importantly *why*.